GIRL DEFIANT

Caribbean Romance and Danger
Book Three

Jonathan Ross

Also by Jonathan Ross

Stand-Alone
Death in a Carolina Swamp
The Jumbee's Daughter
Scent of Death
Reluctant Host

Island Series
New Girl on the Island (Book One)
Stranger on the Island (Book Two)
Stowaway on the Island (Book Three)

Caribbean Romance and Danger Series
Sailor Take Warning (Book One)
Passing in the Night (Book Two)
Girl Defiant (Book Three)

For more information about Jonathan Ross and his novels, please visit www.jonathanrossnovels.com

Information in the following story about West Indies spiritual beliefs reflects some of what the author has learned and some of what he has conjectured. All are recounted with respect.

August 1, 2025

Published by High Ground Initiatives, Arnold, MD USA

Cover Designed by Earthly Charms

Acknowledgments

With grateful thanks to Cheryl Morgan, Donna Baronti, Dorothy Shiffler, Christine O'Connor, and Doug O'Connor for their careful read and valuable comments on the draft manuscript.

CHAPTER 1

Angela froze at the sound – hollow, and barely audible above the comforting night-time chatter of insects and frogs.

It wasn't sharp, like a branch falling onto the corrugated iron roof of her little bungalow home, or scratchy like the wind-blown sand of the crescent beach, or the wispy brush of palm fronds.

It was a dull sound, furtive. A single thump.

She waited by the stove in a corner of the front room, hand poised to light it the moment her boyfriend, Jean, arrived – because he would be hungry. He had called twenty minutes ago and said he'd moored his boat and was on his way.

He would stop at Le Gosier for a bottle of Sancerre, her favorite wine. She would serve him *steak-frites*, his favorite –

Bump!

Again – the same as before. But closer? It sounded nothing like Jean's footsteps.

She grasped a butcher's knife and, motionless, stared at the front door, scanned the windows, shivering as she recalled a grisly murder years ago. It had happened fifty meters outside her bungalow. After the victim – the owner of the house – died, he haunted the bungalow as a zombie. He was a fright, whether viewed through the eyes of her normal human form or her shape-shifted form as a black cat. The zombie was also a grouch who made noise to scare off the living. But he had since passed on to whatever netherworld zombies inhabited, leaving the bungalow blessedly quiet and at peace.

Angela cocked her head, listened, and decided to investigate. She drew a breath and eased out the front door to the porch, her sweaty fingers tight around the knife's handle. She knew a knife would be useless against a zombie, but what she'd heard didn't seem like a zombie sound. They preferred drawn-out mumbling or mysterious scraping, anything to put your hair on end and make you shake all over.

Whatever.

Angela shut the door behind her and stood still, letting her eyes acclimate to the darkness. The moon had risen, throwing its golden beam across the water of her cove, its light revealing palm fronds gently swaying in the Caribbean breeze and outlining the wooden planks of the narrow porch, and stairs down to the yard.

No thumps.

A corner of the bungalow's roof caught her attention. It slanted downward, detached from its broken support post.

Suddenly, a coconut rolled down the slant, thumped onto the porch planking, shuddered, and rolled into two others.

They must have been up there, weighing down the rotten corner structure until it gave way.

Merde. What a ninny I am! Frightened by coconuts. She returned to the kitchen, replaced the knife in its drawer, and tapped her foot impatiently.

Where is Jean?

It was all well and good to be in a serious relationship with the dashing captain of Guadeloupe's Maritime Gendarmerie armed patrol boat LA VIOLETTE, but it was not at all romantic for him to be at sea all the time. He was due for some serious hugs and kisses, that was for sure. She felt a tingle, and grinned at the thought of having him all to herself till morning. She'd have to hide his phone under a pillow – let all those pirates, smugglers, and ship-wrecked sailors wait for him.

From the near distance came the rumble of an approaching car. She ran to the porch, down the steps, to the palms bordering the beach.

An old blue Renault pulled up. Jean!

He jumped out, smiled broadly, and hefted a bottle of wine like a prize.

She rushed to him, kissed him, and hugged him tightly, relishing his strong embrace, his scent.

The wine bottle thudded onto the sand.

She caught her breath. “About time they gave you a little shore leave.”

He held her hand. “I told the commodore if he didn’t let me see you, you’d be banging on the front gate at the base, giving them what for.”

“Did he laugh?”

“No. But he believed me. A week at sea is a long time for the officers and crew of LA VIOLETTE.”

She noticed his breath turning a little ragged.

“Are you hungry? I’m making *steak-frites*.”

He squeezed her close and she felt his muscled body, head to toe and in between.

He whispered, *“Ma chère*, I suggest dinner can wait.”

She sniggered, and led him inside.

CHAPTER 2

Afterward, sitting on Angela's front steps, Jean savored every bite of her *steak-frites* and each sip of Sancerre, but most of all he savored being with Angela. Her smile, how she walked, how she touched him. He thought about her always, especially during long nights at sea. She was the person he came home to, so much better than his lonesome bachelor apartment. He was becoming more and more sure he wanted to marry her and have kids.

But he worried about the constant tug-of-war between life and career. He decided that choosing life – his and Angela's – was the right choice. A sea breeze carried her scent to him. He hugged her and she snuggled close.

His phone buzzed with the distinctive ring tone he'd set for official calls.

He listened for a moment, then swore.

Angela grumped, "*Merde*! I knew I should have hidden that damned phone."

He arrived on the dark Maritime Gendarmerie base and made his way to the pier, where LA VIOLETTE was berthed, bathed in pier lighting and the sounds of preparation.

His first officer, the chief petty officer, and the almost all the rest of the crew were already on board and at their stations. Only one crewman was missing, a machinist mate who lived way up on the north side of Grande-Terre, the larger semi-island of Guadeloupe, and he was due any minute.

Line handlers stood ready on the pier. By the time Jean reached the flying bridge, the machinist mate had clambered aboard. The gangway was raised and stowed. Jean described their mission on the announcing system, heard throughout the vessel. "We're answering a distress call from a motor yacht off the west side of Basse-Terre. There are no details yet, so we need to prepare for fire, flooding, or a search for survivors if the boat sinks before we arrive."

Jean leaned over the port side of the flying bridge, checked that all was clear around pier and within the adjoining harbor.

"Retrieve bow line, retrieve stern line," he commanded. Then to his helmsman, "All ahead slow, right twenty degrees rudder."

Line handlers on the pier slipped the mooring lines from their cleats, and their partners on LA VIOLETTE pulled the freed lines onboard and stowed them.

The helmsman at his midship station on the flying bridge replied, "Aye-aye, sir. All ahead slow, right twenty degrees rudder."

Diesel engines rumbled, and the patrol boat LA VIOLETTE (P 722) eased her nose into the harbor and passed into the dark, rolling Caribbean Sea.

Jean was joined by his first officer, the person second in command of the vessel, Lieutenant (junior grade) Georges Garnier. He was the only one on board with a beard—grown, Jean was sure, to make him look older. Jean pointed out a passenger ship on the horizon and a sportfish five kilometers to the south, although knowing Georges, he had already spotted both vessels.

The man saluted and stood beside Jean at the chest-high forward bulwark of the flying bridge. "All secure for sea, sir, fore and aft."

"Very well."

"It's a good night for it – starry skies, a cool breeze, and nice one-meter rollers."

"Beats a desk job any day of the week."

They grew silent – Jean, Georges, and the helmsman – as LA VIOLETTE sped south, carving a phosphorescent wake. At length, they turned to starboard, around the looming and shadowed volcanic Basse-Terre, the western semi-island of Guadeloupe. Jean ordered an initial north-westerly course toward the estimated location of the vessel in distress.

He leaned down and spoke into the intercom, connected to the radar watch on the enclosed bridge, one deck below. "Any sighting?"

"Yes, sir, just coming on radar. About ten kilometers to the northwest. Must be him – there's no other traffic out there."

"Good. Give me a course to intercept."

"Aye, sir. She's dead in the water. Course to intercept is three-one-zero."

Jean turned to the helmsman. "Make your course three-one-zero."

The helmsman adjusted heading and the vessel heeled onto her new course.

Ten minutes later, Georges lowered his Thales O-Nyx night vision binoculars and pointed toward a yellow dot in the distance. "I've got her."

Jean raised his binoculars and found the vessel, rolling in the seas, dead in the water. As they approached, the boat's light grew in size, glowing and undulating, one moment sharp and the next clouded over.

"She's on fire!" Jean said, and ordered the helmsman, "Make your speed twenty-eight knots. Sound general quarters, call out boarding party with fire assistance. Prepare to launch the rigid inflatable."

"Aye-aye, sir. Twenty-eight knots, GQ, fire assist boarding, and launch RIB."

LA VIOLETTE responded, her engines roaring, deck plates quivering, and bow surging into swells. Jean gripped the bulwark, catching only glimpses of the burning vessel through his gyrating binoculars.

At a distance of two hundred meters, Jean ordered speed reduced to five knots. No binoculars were needed to determine the vessel was a seaworthy sportfish yacht about twenty-five meters in length, its cabin engulfed in flames. Three arm-waving men stood at the transom on the aft deck, as far from the fire's heat as possible.

Jean maneuvered LA VIOLETTE closer, pausing when they were fifty meters upwind of the yacht. He noticed there were no running lights showing and felt a pang of suspicion. His suspicion increased when he examined the three-man crew, dressed in work clothes and not the usual shorts and t-shirts of yacht owners and their guests. What's more, they appeared oddly subdued, quite the opposite of the usual jumping, hugging, and non-stop chattering of people just rescued at sea.

There was a loud pop inside the cabin and the flames increased, leaping out the side windows, cracking the bits of remaining glass. The crew jumped over the transom and knelt on the swim platform, casting frightened looks up at LA VIOLETTE.

"They probably can't swim," Georges offered. "Kinda strange they don't look all that happy to see us."

"Smugglers," said Jean, examining them again with binoculars.

Georges muttered, "Should we send an armed boarding party? They aren't even pretending to fight the fire."

"Yes," Jean said, and to the helmsman, "Belay fire assistance and order armed boarding party to the RIB. Man both machine guns to cover our crew. Keep fire assistance on standby."

Jean placed his binoculars in the case attached to bulwark and stepped to the ladder, saying, "Mr. Garnier has the deck and the conn. I'm going with the RIB."

He descended to the main deck and trotted aft. He took his bullet-proof vest, life jacket, and side arm from the chief petty officer, and joined the well-armed men seating themselves on the RIB.

The three men on the yacht remained kneeling on the swim platform, gazing with grim expressions at the approaching RIB. One pointed at LA VIOLETTE's two mounted machineguns aimed in their direction and one of the others looked and shook his head sadly. The third, his face hard, glared at Jean.

The RIB bumped the hull of the burning boat and Jean noticed a tart smell to the smoke. He stared into the eyes of the third man, obviously the leader.

"We are coming aboard. Stand back, place your hands where we can see them."

The man shrugged. Jean nodded to his team lead, who translated to Spanish, which the three men understrood, immediately complying. Jean's other two team members aimed their weapons, keeping fingers outside the trigger guards, but ready for action.

Jean and his team boarded the burning vessel, keeping the three men covered. Jean saw that the fire had not yet fully spread to the outside of the structure, but was fast consuming furnishings inside the cabin.

The windscreen up forward broke with a loud crack.

Jean turned to his RIB driver. “Return in the RIB for the fire assistance.”

“Aye sir.”

Jean’s team motioned for the yacht crew to joint them on the aft deck, where they were frisked for arms and cuffed, then told to sit on deck with their backs against the transom.

Jean and his men sniffed, and one of the men said, “I think it’s drugs.”

“I agree,” Jean said, eyeing the cabin and then his prisoners.

The RIB returned and four crewmen climbed aboard the yacht, passing up fire extinguishers and two axes. They moved forward as a team and extinguished the fire.

The team lead reported to Jean, “The fire was contained inside the cabin – couch, chairs, carpet. Lucky it didn’t get to the fuel. I suspect it was a galley fire.”

Jean nodded, then glanced at the scowling man who appeared to be the leader, and the other two, staring at the deck, looking afraid.

Casualties of a seemingly unending drug war.

CHAPTER 3

Angela awoke in the gray pre-dawn, lonely and jumpy. At first she thought the feelings arose from Jean having to leave early. She'd missed him these past few days and had looked forward to time together. Special time.

She shook her head.

Jean's early departure was disappointing, but something else bothered her.

She pulled on shorts and top and strode along the beach. The gentle pre-dawn breeze caressed her arms and cheeks, the lapping waves were their musical selves. But the dark mood remained stubbornly in place.

Back in her bungalow, she munched egg and toast, gulped coffee, then left to tread the winding, sandy path between her cove and the marina where she kept her sloop.

She walked past the machinery-repair workshop, its door still locked. She'd made friends with the mechanic, Michel, a gentle man in his fifties, hair going white. He was a good mechanic and a comfortable friend, a person to share island gossip with, who didn't give her advice. Well, unless she asked, and then it was modestly doled out, leaving no doubt that she was in charge of her decisions.

Angela stepped onto the wooden pier, slippery from the early-morning dew, and checked all the boats. This was her third week working at the marina, a part-time job that paid her mooring fee plus a bit left over, helping to conserve the money she'd carefully set aside for her post-university adventure. Her work duties included slip rentals, boat repair invoicing, refueling visiting boats, facility maintenance, and other administrative odd jobs as they arose. The pace was slow, as with everything on the islands.

Angela knew the cloudy mood settling into her chest was not caused by job pressures. Nor was it a case of personal animosities. She got on well with Michel, as with the marina owner, and the owners of all the boats.

Except she had not yet met the owner of the newest boat, tied to the pier farthest from the workshop, and farthest from the shore. Usually, that was the least popular berth, because it was closest to the sea and the longest walk from the parking lot for carrying stuff. Anyone assigned to it readily moved when a berth became available closer to shore. Yet the owner of the newest boat chose that berth over two others that were closer in. Michel had dealt with the man, and Angela had yet to meet him, but that choice had struck her as curious.

Nearing the end of her morning inspection, she approached his boat, a ratty-looking island-made fishing vessel of wood construction. It looked like an elongated row boat, with a low cabin amidships and open decks fore and aft. It was about ten meters long, and its wide beam and mildly-raked bow made it appear seaworthy in spite of its flat sides.

She reached the boat and paused, puzzled by the boat itself as much as with its owner's choice of berth. She found it weird that the inboard engine with its boxy cover was so large that it dominated the deck space inside the cabin. In addition, it was a gasoline engine – very odd indeed. First, because boats of this size invariably used outboard motors for propulsion, and second, because boats with inboard engines were almost always fitted with diesel engines, not gas. Gas was for speed, and this boat was not built for speed.

Angela scowled at the flaking paint, the sloppy mooring lines. And the rudder, which was attached to the flat transom, like on a Caribbean sloop. Why wasn't it mounted beneath the hull, just behind the propeller?

There was something else she couldn't quite put her finger on, until she noticed the dew beaded up on the roof of the cabin and the top of the engine cover. She leaned over the dock, and discovered that thin gray sheeting was attached to not only those two areas but almost all flat surfaces above the waterline.

Shrugging away these curious bits and pieces, she noticed that the hull was heeling twenty degrees to port. Worse, water sloshed above the deck planking, in time with the gentle swells.

Flooding!

Even more alarming were two legs protruding from the gap between engine cover and the port-side inner hull.

Man's legs, flat on the deck.

"Hey!" she shouted, kneeling and staring at the unmoving legs. "Are you okay?"

No answer, but the legs shook vigorously, and she jumped aboard, the boat sluggishly rolling from her added weight. She waded through ankle-deep water on the aft deck, stepped forward, stooped, and entered the cabin.

She stared aghast at a man, face-down on the deck, his legs and body half-submerged in water.

With obvious effort, the man raised his shoulders and turned his head, spit out water, coughed, and said. "She's sinking!"

The man's nose was barely above water. Both his arms extended downward into swirling blackness.

She shifted to the starboard side, and the boat heeled. Water flowed away from the man and over her shoes.

He yelled, "For god sake, do something! I'm stuck and the damned boat is sinking!"

Angela cast around for something heavy to counter-balance the boat further to starboard and gain time to work the man free. She found nothing at hand in the boat, and in desperation surveyed the pier.

She spotted five red gasoline cans in a row. Leaping onto the pier, she transferred them to the edge of the pier nearest the boat. All were full, and heavy. She jumped back aboard, reached up and, grunting with effort, positioned them on deck against the starboard hull structure. The vessel now tilted only ten degrees, decreasing the depth of water above the port-side deck. She prayed it was enough to enable the man to breathe while she figured out how to free his arms.

Angela waded back to him, noticing his mouth and nose were raised above the water by a couple of centimeters. But the level continued to rise. She knelt close to him. "How can I help?"

"Roll me outboard. That'll free my right hand. Both my hands are trapped in the piping down below."

She positioned herself in the space between his body and the inner port side of the boat. Grabbing his shoulders and chest, she braced her feet against the engine cover and pulled.

Nothing.

"Keep on," he said, his voice hoarse.

She glanced aft, spied a boat hook. Grabbed it and positioned it as a lever up near his arm pits, the hook resting in a gap in the deck planking, her hands gripping the top. She gently pulled, increasing tension.

"That's it. Keep on."

"Does it hurt?"

"Yeah!" He drew what sounded like a painful breath. "No choice. Keep pulling."

She increased tension, felt him roll slightly, then he cursed and pulled his right arm free.

"*Merde*! Now you can remove the boat hook. Just stand there in case I lose my balance and start to roll back."

He put his right hand on deck, jiggled his left arm, and rose a few centimeters, then farther, clear of the water, which had risen another five centimeters.

"Okay," he said. "Stand clear. I need to reach down and shut a valve before the boat sinks."

She waited, ready in case he got trapped again, but he took a deep breath and reached down with only his right hand. His shoulder muscles tightened, then released, and he rose, dripping water, his long black hair drooping like a blanket around muscled shoulders. She gave him space and he stood, slightly hunched in the low cabin, then gestured aft. She moved to the open aft deck near an ice box.

He joined her, eyes glistening with tension, water trickling from trousers and t-shirt. He reached into the ice box, pulled out a six-pack of beer, handed her one, and kept one for himself. He shut the lid and laid the remaining beers on top.

He gulped his beer, swished it like mouthwash, and spit it over the side, explaining, "I got a mouthful of gasoline. Tastes awful."

He raised his bottle and she followed suit. "To you, *mademoiselle*, for saving my life. I owe you."

Angela drank, and responded, "But you don't owe me, *monsieur*. I am sure you would have done the same for me. We are sailors."

He wiped his face and studied her, his eyes probing, brow furrowed, muscles now tensed and tendons tight, like ropes in a squall.

She swallowed hard, remembering her dark mood earlier.

Was it a warning?

If so, of this man's dangerous plight – or of the man himself?

He broke the silence, his voice menacing. "Do you know who I am?"

She waited a beat, resolved not to be bullied by a man who should have been grateful.

"No, we have not met. Michel took your information. I assume you are the owner of this boat."

He nodded, as if he had forgotten something, and changed the subject. "Yes, I am the owner. I came to inspect my boat and saw that she was low in the water. I opened the access panel to the bilge pump and discovered a valve had been opened, allowing water to enter the bilges. I needed both hands to twist the valve because it was corroded." He shrugged. "But to reach it, I found myself with both arms wedged tight, stuck in the access opening."

"With no one around."

"Yes, and a death by drowning about two minutes away." He swigged the rest of his beer and stared at her again, this time gently, like a brother. "My name is Vincent Ballou."

Angela was at first disconcerted by his abrupt mood changes, but after a moment's reflection she figured that facing such a horrible death would put anyone off balance, even a man as tough as he appeared to be.

She extended her hand. "I'm Angela Spencer. I help out here at the marina."

"Enchantée de vous rencontrer."

They shook.

"Your hand is cold, Vincent. We must sit in the sun."

He gave her an odd look, nodded, and they moved to the pier, where they sat, legs dangling over the side, the boat rocking serenely in the marina cove. He rubbed his hands and smiled. "I remember your name now, from my friend Emilie. You are a kind person, one of the people who help protect the sea turtles."

"Yes."

"Well, Angela Spencer, I am not such a kind person. I am the leader of the Dockers."

"The gang."

"Yes." She looked at his boat, remembered the engine – gasoline and oversized. Which meant the boat was probably used to smuggle drugs, disguised as just another island fishing boat. It was 'invisible' to police, but possessed the speed and range to transit to other islands. And this man was indeed dangerous. But, she was convinced, not to her.

He gave her a knowing smile, as if reading her thoughts.

She chose her words carefully. "Do you think it was sabotage?"

"Yes. Another gang keeps its boat here as well."

"I imagine you would prefer that I do not call the police."

His eyes flashed darkly. "The police must not be involved. It is a situation I will address myself."

"What will you do?"

"I must think."

"We – Michel and I – do prefer a peaceful marina."

"Without a gang war."

"Er, yes."

"We shall see." He extended his hand, and his grip was gentle. "*Au revoir*, Angela Spencer. Thank you for saving my life. I am in your debt."

CHAPTER 4

Estelle Boucher exited the Metro at Sully-Morland station and ascended the stairs, emerging into the cool Paris morning. She headed south on a familiar route, crossing over the Seine on Pont de Sully Bridge to the Left Bank. She continued briefly down the tree-shaded quay, then jay-walked across Quai de la Tournelle, snarled with rush-hour traffic.

Gaining the sidewalk on the other side, lined with luxurious old-world apartments, she spared a glance at the august halls of Sorbonne Universite UPMC. She recalled her intense education at the famous university. Reluctantly, she admitted that she had earned a bookish credibility from her efforts, if not practical knowledge.

Her thoughts turned to the person she was hurrying to meet – her Aunt Sabrina Abon. The woman, like Estelle, was born and raised in a wealthy family on French Guadeloupe. Also, like Estelle, she had departed the island under a dark cloud.

She was Estelle's only true friend, having remained loyal during Estelle's lonely banishment to a Swiss finishing school. Afterward, Aunt Sabrina had invited her to stay in Paris, becoming her mentor and teaching her how to experience life in a way Estelle had never imagined.

What Estelle had learned from Aunt Sabrina gave her the ability to move in the highest circles of Parisian society, business, and politics. Most importantly, she learned how to manipulate a person into doing what was best for her while making them believe it was all about what was best for them.

At the entrance to her aunt's apartment building, Estelle pressed the intercom buzzer. She self-consciously straightened her scarf, the one her aunt said complimented her coloring. She jangled her bracelet, which was modest, as were her jeans and white-and-black striped t-shirt. Only her blue blazer, keeping her warm in the morning breeze, was from a Parisian designer, providing an accent of elegance.

It all added up to creating a first impression, Estelle reflected. Which seemed silly at first, especially because she and her aunt were relatives and the best of friends. They saw each other often. It would be logical to ignore her aunt's 'first impression' dictate.

Yet the subject at hand this morning was of monumental importance, and as with any human endeavor, it would begin with a first impression. 'Setting the stage for what followed,' as her aunt would say.

This morning, Estelle needed Aunt Sabrina to view her as a professional in the realm of accumulating and exercising power. To overdress was to convey a lack of confidence. To underdress showed a lack of appreciation for the gravity of the issue at hand. Estelle had chosen chic informal.

The speaker pulled her back to the present.

"*Oui? C'est toi*, Estelle ?"

Estelle smiled politely, even though there was no video. "Yes, it is me, Aunt Sabrina. Good morning."

"Good morning, my dear Estelle."

The door lock buzzed and Estell entered the building. She felt a tingling in her chest, as if signaling that this final portion of her morning journey foreshadowed ascendance to the next plateau of her career.

The elevator, recently refurbished, whispered its way to the third level, and a moment later Aunt Sabrina responded to Estelle's gentle knock and opened her apartment door. Estelle smiled to herself, because her aunt had obviously sensed the importance of their meeting, and had herself honored the 'good first impression' rule.

Estelle took in her aunt's modest black skirt with a thin white leather belt, a blue-patterned long-sleeve blouse, and a Hermes scarf at her neck. The scarf being her note of elegance. She appeared to wear only lipstick, though Estelle knew she also wore just a little makeup and a bit of blusher on her cheeks. The impression was a woman of confidence and elegance.

They traded double cheek kisses and entered the foyer, Estelle marveling at her aunt's seamless continuation past first impressions. Even her invitation to come to her living room was full of endearing grace, with a gentle gesture toward Estelle's usual seat.

It was a Louis XV chair, one of a pair. According to Sabrina, it was designed for comfort, including the option of sitting back comfortably. Its cushioning was decorated by a floral scene of birds, deer, and flowers. Estelle tried sitting back, placing her hands on the padded arm rests. A second later, she found herself leaning forward, as if entranced in the final scene of a tense opera, to signal to her aunt that what they were about to discuss was important. She clasped her hands in her lap to keep them still.

Seeking calm in which to gather her thoughts, she gazed at the large painting dominating the wall opposite from where she sat. It depicted two women, a young man, and an infant, languidly fishing in a woods. The original was painted by commission to King Louis XV and hung in Grand Trianon in Versailles. It was the only reproduction piece in Sabrina's apartment.

Everything else was original, which usually made Estelle feel like a cossetted princess. But today, the historic grandeur kept her on edge – the perfection in design and execution mocked the flaws that she was certain lurked in her proposed scheme.

Aunt Sabrina swept in from the kitchen, bearing a silver tray with coffee service. She sat opposite Estelle on a magnificent couch and set the tray on a coffee table. She poured coffee and passed Estelle her cup and saucer. Estelle added sugar, took an appreciative sip, and set the coffee down with an unwelcome tremor.

Sabrina did the same, though with her usual aplomb, and adjusted the hem of her skirt to sit just above her knee. Estelle nodded in appreciation. Her best friend and mentor had managed to seat her guest comfortably, gifted her with an opportunity to catch her breath, and presented a wonderful tray of coffee and light pastries. It was ordinary hospitality but delivered with disarming elegance.

Sabrina now leaned forward and made eye contact. "Tell me, dear Estelle. What is the occasion? You are wonderfully dressed for an informal get together and you arrived precisely two minutes after ten o'clock, which is to say you gave your hostess time to take care of last-minute preparations."

Estelle smiled. "Am I not your star apprentice?"

"You are a dream. You have become a desirable woman – professionally, intellectually, and erotically, and have taken the younger generation of diplomats and businessmen by storm. You are the darling of the ball."

"My gosh, what a compliment! Thank you, Aunt Sabrina."

"Well, it's time to recognize your achievements over these past months. You have a bright future as a power behind the scenes, exercising your wit and charm to make things happen."

"Thanks again."

"You are welcome. By the way, did I sense urgency in your call?"

Estelle's mouth went dry. She sipped coffee.

Sabrina glanced at her with a gentle smile, and Estelle took the cue. It helped, but only a little. The plan she had devised was the boldest she had ever dreamt of.

"I have come for your advice, of course. It is about the next large step in my advancement."

Sabrina's eyes widened. "Ah, yes! Your own idea. A worthy scheme?"

"Yes. It involves an initiative between France and Mexico, and includes diplomats and police on both sides. Very hush-hush."

It was Sabrina's turn to place a trembling coffee cup and saucer on the table. "*Mon Dieu*, dear Estelle!"

"I realize it could be dangerous."

"It could be deadly. Anything at that level carries special risks."

"Yes. I am frightened but I am also excited."

"Like a hunter who realizes she might become the hunted?"

"I guess."

"Consider wisely, my dear. But enough advice. You are your own person. Tell me your thoughts."

"Okay, but first I have a question. Have you heard of Operation Kingfish?"

"Hmm. Yes, the name. And a scrap of information – that it is international in nature."

"Yes, it is the name of a French-Mexican initiative, and even this name, 'Operation Kingfish', is highly sensitive. I beg you to treat that and all aspects of our conversation today with utmost discretion."

"You have my word."

"Aunt Sabrina, you are the only person I trust with what I have so far learned, and what I propose to do."

"I am now on the edge of my seat, my dear."

Estelle chuckled. "Okay. I am supporting Maurice on this project, which has been his main focus for several weeks."

"Maurice?"

"Yes, my mentor, boss, and lover." They exchanged knowing looks and Angela continued, "Maurice works for Charles Bernard. But more of that later."

Sabrina's eyes sparkled. "Ah, Charles. He is a charmer. Too young for me, but ambitious. Worthy for your attention."

Estelle tilted her head and her aunt made motions of zipping her lips closed.

"Maurice has included me in the operation's planning, which will next progress to a group meeting of French diplomats, followed by a project kick-off meeting that includes our Mexican counterparts."

"And you will attend both meetings?"

Estelle made a face. "The first meeting, yes, and that is part of my plan. But not the second meeting."

"Oh dear. Does Maurice get to go to that second one?"

"From rumors I have heard, yes, representing Charles' group. But I will definitely not be invited."

Sabrina smirked.

"You are correct, Aunt Sabrina. Boudoir pillow talk has already provided me with more details. There is a certain person of interest at the center of the operation, and he is Mexican. The police have his home under constant surveillance."

"Awaiting the word to swoop down and capture him?"

"Yes."

"Hmm, let me guess. You are growing bored of Maurice and wish to align yourself with a bigger fish. Say, for example, Charles, who, by the way, is a rising star in France. He's been posted in the leading capitals of Europe and the Americas.

"His present assignment is powerful, his contacts legion, and he possesses the ability to make the worst blunder go away. I seem to remember that he was with a black operations department a while back. The man is being groomed for higher things."

Estelle felt the heat of a blush, surprised at the accuracy of her aunt's deduction that she, Estelle, was switching horses.

Sabrina laughed. "It is the sort of twist that I expect of you, my dear Estelle. I trust that you have kept your wits about you when you are with these men, especially if you are in the same room with both of them."

"I've been the model of decorum, and have only joined Charles for cocktails, nothing more intimate."

"You arranged for him to invite you?"

"I asked for his help in writing a position paper."

"Good, nurturing the personal side of your relationship with him under the guise of the professional side. Plus, in asking for his help, you are caressing his ego. How did that work for you?"

"He did give me advice. We discussed options, and I ended up with a lot more information than I needed for the paper. I learned what his opinions were regarding a number of aspects of Operation Kingfish, including legal procedures, international norms, and police tactics."

"Perhaps he mentioned that the Mexican police can be brutal. They make people disappear and others die in custody."

Estelle shrugged. "We do the same in France. A nation guards its power jealously. Anyway, Mexico and France have had enough of this person of interest."

"So, you aim to add a twist to Operation Kingfish and become an associate of Charles?"

"Yes."

"What happens to Maurice?"

Angela pictured the man – tall, thin, and ascetic, with wire-rim glasses. Intelligent, ambitious, but plodding.

She said, "He will find himself without an assistant."

"And lover," Sabrina murmured thoughtfully. "That could make you an enemy."

"So, I am employing your advice."

Sabrina smiled. “By the nature of our profession, you will make enemies, so you must be sure your next mentor is more powerful than the one you spurn, and he will protect you.”

“Right. Charles is much more powerful than Maurice, and if my scheme works, the credit for correcting a flaw in the execution of Operation Kingfish will be given to Charles. He will come out the hero, and he will know full well that the credit is really mine, so I will ride his coattails as he ascends to a higher level. Also, the blame will be borne by Maurice. Charles will allow Maurice to save face by transferring to another department where he will have no professional contact with Charles or me.”

“Will he bear a grudge?”

Estelle frowned. “Maurice? Oh yes, his ego is huge and he never forgets an insult. He would be a continuing danger to keep track of.”

“Well said. Now, down to practicalities.”

“First I must gain further information from the French-Mexican meeting, at the Mexican embassy here in Paris. Then I can perfect my plan. But one element seems clear, given the partnership between France and Mexico, and that is the need for instant availability of transportation between the two countries and with Guadeloupe. Time will be of the essence.”

“Ah, transportation. You require the use of a private airplane.”

“Yes. Do you know how I might go about obtaining one for a week or so, with sufficient range to cross the Atlantic?”

“Hmm, private jets do cross the Atlantic, stopping to refuel along the way or being fitted with extra fuel tanks.”

“It would need to be a special arrangement. ‘Under the radar,’ I believe is the expression.”

“Of course. Utmost discretion. I have a contact who has no love for our country. Word of this flaw would eventually leak, and my contact would be delighted to have tweaked the pride of France. Shall I call him?”

“Aunt Sabrina, that would be most helpful.”

“You must realize that the loan of his airplane comes with a price. He will contact you at some time in the future, asking you for a favor.”

“Yes, you have taught me – there is always a price.”

CHAPTER 5

Towing the fire-gutted, drug-smugglers' boat took the rest of the night and all of the following morning. Jean, remaining on the flying bridge the whole time, was tempted to cut the tow line and sink the damned vessel, but he knew the authorities ashore wanted to check for hidden drugs and various clues that might identify the boss of the syndicate behind the smuggling.

So, he remained topside, available in case of emergency. He'd chased his first officer away to get a few hours' sleep. Now, he squinted into the mid-morning sun, checked the seas, and felt the subtle tug of the smugglers' boat, trailing behind.

He turned at the sound of approaching footsteps on deck and smiled at his first officer, looking refreshed and bearing two cups of steaming coffee.

"You're a sight for sore eyes, Georges."

"Thanks, captain." He handed Jean a coffee. "I thought you could use a morning boost of energy. Looks like we're most of the way up Bass-Terre." He gestured toward the mountainous land, five kilometers off the port side.

Jean nodded and said, "I got another call from the commodore."

"My condolences."

Jean grunted, which meant he agreed that his boss was a micro-manager but could not directly say so because it would be breaking military etiquette.

Georges sipped his coffee, waited a moment, then tentatively asked, "Permission to speak frankly, sir?"

Jean trusted his second in command, formerly a chief petty officer, then commissioned to his present rank. The man was experienced and savvy. "Go ahead, Georges."

"You might already know all this, but Lieutenant-Commander Kingsley Lavigne – our commodore – almost ruined the reputation of LA VIOLETTE when he was captain of our valiant patrol boat. I have heard that he was kicked upstairs so a new skipper could be assigned.

Jean remained silent.

"You," Georges said.

"I figured that's what had happened. We both remember the rock-bottom state of moral back then. *Mon Dieu*, I felt like I'd just entered a prison. No one talked, no eye contact, and little things kept being left undone."

Georges nodded. "Right, sir. And turnover was brutal. We spent all our time training new guys, who immediately requested a transfer and we had to start again. But what I wanted to say is that you changed all that. You earned their trust – beginning with me and the chief, and then the crew, when you treated them as human beings and not slaves."

"Thanks, Georges. You – and they – are the best. The A-Team."

"It starts at the top, captain, especially on a small boat like ours. I had one other thing to say."

"Okay."

"Be careful today when you meet with the commodore. He is up to more than micro-managing, sir. I believe he's got a wild hair up his ass about something big."

"Now that you mention it, I think you're right. That would be the real reason he ordered me to report to his office the moment we moored."

"It'll have something to do with his career."

"Often the case with senior officers."

"Right, and he's about as high as he can get, except for a transfer to one of the groups in France."

"Which is not likely."

"Yup. Needs his ticket punched along the way, and that's pretty difficult if you're in a small outfit like ours. I'm thinking he'll try to charm you into thinking he's doing you a favor, when he's really flushing you down the shitter."

"You know, you swear like a chief when you're mad."

"Yes, sir."

Jean drew a breath. "Georges, I value your advice most of anyone aboard. I trust your instincts – as a chief and as an officer. Thanks for giving me the straight skinny."

"You're welcome. Just one more thing."

"What?"

"The crew and I, well, we're not allowing you to accept any other assignment. You're our skipper and we damned want it to stay that way. Sir."

Jean grinned. "Georges, you are amazing."

"Yes, sir."

After LA VIOLETTE was secured at her pier, and after a quick shave and change into a clean uniform, Jean trotted to the administrative headquarters building and ascended the stairs to the commodore's office.

Georges' words about the commodore having an agenda made perfect sense. Even before placing the smugglers' boat under tow, Jean had fully briefed the commodore from LA VIOLETTE, then he updated him when he called back again. The commodore did not need a face-to-face meeting for what had been a routine mission. Jean mentally shrugged – the man was always pushing, always impatient.

The commodore's yeoman, at his desk in an anteroom, greeted Jean with a salute and gestured toward the closed door to the commodore's office.

"Go right on in, sir. He's expecting you."

"Thanks."

Jean knocked twice and entered the large office, containing a conference table, shelves with books and mementos from the commodore's career, a couple of photos on the walls, of the commodore with various dignitaries, and a large, government-issued desk, behind which the commodore sat, his back straight, head down.

Jean stood at attention in front of the desk, ignoring the two visitor's chairs, and saluted.

"Reporting as ordered, commodore."

The commodore straightened, scowled, and returned the salute. “Glad you could make it.”

Which sounded a lot like, ‘it took you long enough.’

He motioned to a chair and Jean sat, curious and fully alert.

The commodore seemed to gather his thoughts, arranging papers into three neat stacks and minutely adjusting the framed picture of his wife and two kids. He looked out the window toward the harbor, filled with nautical traffic.

At length, he cleared his throat and asked, “Do you have anything else to report regarding last night’s incident, in addition to what you told me earlier?”

Jean answered, “No sir, except that the smugglers seemed pretty surprised to have been rescued by the Maritime Gendarmerie and not the Coast Guard.”

“Hmph, we are the Coast Guard. That’s our main duty.”

“I guess no one told them. They just called the emergency frequency on their radio. Too bad for them.”

“Did you get any intelligence from them on the way back?”

“No, sir. The Spanish-speakers guarding them reported that the men whispered to each other for a minute or two, then shut up tight. Not a word. I suspect their leader ordered them to remain silent.”

“Right. Where’s their boat now?”

“Moored behind us at our pier, available for inspection. She’s not taking on water, so there’s no danger of sinking.”

“Alright. I’ve notified my liaison with the city drug-enforcement police. They’ll get back to me on arrangements to visit the vessel and secure any drugs or other evidence.”

The commodore reached to the nearest stack of papers and removed what looked like an official message. Although, from his angle, Jean could not tell exactly what it was.

The commodore said, “I received this last night. It’s highly sensitive. Are you cleared for Top Secret?”

Which was an odd question, because all at-sea commanding officers were cleared at that level, granting them access to highly classified data that affected French national security, counterterrorism, and counterintelligence.

“Yes, sir,” I have a TS clearance.

The commodore grunted, sounding disappointed. "According to this, you do have a need-to-know."

Again, the disappointed tone.

The commodore studied the page. "There will be a meeting in Paris. I have to believe it involves drugs and Guadeloupe, and in particular, the seas surrounding our islands." His lips quirked. "During the meeting you will likely be assigned a role."

Jean nodded.

The commodore asked, "Are you in a position to travel for up to a week? No obligations here that could hold you back?"

"My only obligation is as captain of LA VIOLETTE."

The commodore gestured dismissively. "Yes, of course. Your first officer can take charge in your absence."

"Yes, sir, he is completely qualified in all respects."

Which earned him a look, and Jean figured the man considered only himself capable of making such a judgement. He looked Jean in the eye.

"I want you to be sure there is no cause for you to remain here. There is no problem, either professional or personal?"

Jean nearly laughed – it was as if a visit to Paris was a terrible disruption to his life. The obvious sought-after response was 'yes, there is a problem. I should really stay here, as should my first officer.' Then the commodore would attempt to attend the Paris meeting and mingle with senior officers, widen his circle of contacts, and better his position for promotion.

It was just as Georges had predicted.

Jean maintained a straight face and serious tone. "*Merci beaucoup*, commodore, for your consideration. But since it appears that I have been assigned the task through this notice you hold, then I should carry through in a professional manner. And to confirm, I am not constrained."

The commodore frowned, obviously frustrated. "There will be civilian diplomats at the meeting along with military and police officials. The meeting itself is highly classified and will occur as a brief interlude during a reception at the Mexican embassy.

"The reception is nominally in honor of a minor diplomatic event which both France and Mexico recognize. Everyone will wear civilian attire, and not too formal at that. It's a 'simple summer cocktails and tapas occasion.' In fact, do not take your uniform at all. Your orders are to comport yourself in Paris as a tourist on holiday." He paused, as if for emphasis, and added with a chagrined look, "It is suggested that you bring a companion. All the better, I assume, to make the trip appear unofficial."

Jean maintained his composure only with the greatest effort. *My gosh, a vacation in Paris for Angela and me. She will be swept off her feet!* Glancing at the commodore's continuing frown, Jean realized that if the man were to take Jean's place, he would invite his wife. He was losing a personal and a professional opportunity. No wonder he was upset.

"Yes sir. I understand. Civilian tourists."

The commodore pursed his lips. "Exactly. We'll take care of all expenses. The meeting will only last an hour or so. It is our first face-to-face with Mexico for a program, codename: Operation Kingfish."

Jean blinked, mystified at the Mexican connection and the high level of secrecy. Most of all, he wondered about the purpose of the operation. Obviously too delicate to include in the page that now shook in the commodore's hand – likely from anger.

And why the devil didn't the commodore let him read the damned memo?

The man continued, "You should pay a courtesy call to our office in Paris, but what you learn at the Mexican embassy is not to be discussed there. That goes for me as well – I only want to know what I receive officially from our people in Paris."

"So, the French team will brief our Maritime Gendarmerie headquarters as they – the French – deem appropriate – and they will likewise brief you?"

"Yes. You might receive sensitive particulars, you understand?"

"Still, it's a little awkward."

The commodore shrugged, as if the whole affair was of only modest importance. But he abruptly placed the page on one stack of paper and moved another in front of him, and then bid Jean good day with a glare.

CHAPTER 6

Angela was elated that Jean was visiting again, though she prayed his phone would not ring as it did before. They enjoyed carry-out and Sancerre, which they munched as they talked, shoulders touching, sitting on her front steps in the night.

Waves lapped at the beach, a breeze rustled palms, and insects chirped in the night.

She'd never planned on staying on Guadeloupe, but her post-university summer cruise on her dad's sloop had ended there, and happily so. She had fallen in love.

She sipped her wine and held his hand. "Will you remain at the base for a while?"

"No, we're on immediate stand-by, as usual. The next four-day maintenance availability is not for another months."

"That's a long time. Do you want to plan a day at the turtle beach or the rainforest or something?"

"Yes, the 'something' choice perhaps, though we won't exactly be alone."

"Hmm, you have plans. Very mysterious."

He gave her a kiss and grinned. "What would you say to a couple of days in Paris?"

She blinked in disbelief. "Paris? *Mon Dieu*! That would be great. What's the catch?"

He laughed. "You're right – there's always a catch. I've been ordered to attend a special meeting there, which would take several hours. No details given, except for the date, time, and place."

"Wow, even more mysterious."

He nodded, his face solemn in the moonlight. “I think it’s about a major policy change, or a special operation. I’m to wear civilian clothes, no uniform, and I was encouraged to invite my plus-one.”

“So, I’m part of the mystery. And this would be like a vacation except for when you’re at the meeting. Where will you stash me?”

“You can stay at our hotel or explore the city while I’m busy. But we’ll go together to a reception at the Mexican embassy.”

“Good grief! An embassy! Diplomats and important people, all gussied up. Oh-my-gosh! I have nothing to wear.”

“How about your gold earrings?”

She elbowed him. “Right. Me in my gold earrings. How about the other stuff? You know, shoes, dress, accessories.”

“I think you’ll be fine – the reception dress code is ‘Paris street casual,’ which I imagine is not really too dressy.”

“But includes a neck scarf for the ladies?”

He grinned. “I guess.”

“They all wear scarves, even with jeans.”

“Maybe you can look it up on the Internet.”

“I’ll ask around, too. Someone must have visited France in the past few months. Maybe a shopkeeper buying new stock. Anyway, do you think diplomats are capable of dressing down?”

“They’ll have to – it’s part of the invitation, and to impress their host, in this case the Mexican ambassador.”

“And his wife, I’m sure. Yes. Okay, I have an outfit. What about us in Paris? Do they dress up for meals?”

“French women always look like they’ve stepped out of a fashion magazine, and the men do, too, with tailored pants and shirts. I guess I’ll have to buy a few new shirts. Would you help me choose?”

“Sure. Hmm, maybe I’ll borrow a few things from Catherine, too.”

“We can pack lightly,” he said in a hopeful tone.

“Ha, so you say. Even casual means at least three pairs of shoes, plus one for the reception.”

“Shoes are bulky. I only took two pairs when I was in the l'École des Officiers de la Gendarmerie Nationale in France and they seemed to take up half my suitcase.”

“Maybe we could share one big suitcase and each take a carry-on. Would that work?”

He gave her a squeeze. "Sure. Pack two suitcases if you want. All our expenses will be paid by the government. Be sure to include a pair of comfortable shoes because Paris is a walking city, full of sights. I stayed there for a couple of days when I attended the l'École des Officiers."

"I've heard there is a big store with hundreds of perfumes you can test."

"I guess."

"And a fashion district?"

"Well, it is Paris."

"And museums of art, and the Louvre. Let's go to the Louvre while we're there."

"Okay, it'll be our first stop, about ten minutes' walk from our hotel. "

"I'm so excited!" But a sudden thought shattered her enthusiasm – Jean's ex-girlfriend lived in Paris! *Mon Dieu!* A woman so wild that her family banished her to a Swiss finishing school and university. Oh yeah, and she was involved with one of the Guadeloupe's vicious gangs.

With a lump in her throat, Angela asked, "What about Estelle? Will she be at the reception?"

"Probably. She seems to know lots of embassy people, and she's a snoop and social climber, so she might show up."

"Hmph."

He grinned mischievously. "You may at last get a chance to meet her."

"I swear Jean, if that woman makes a pass at you, I'll choke her."

"Are you sure you want to go?"

"Of course I want to go!" She laughed. "I'll have you all to myself for the whole time except for the reception and your meeting. And don't worry, I'll be polite to Estelle. But I still don't like her one bit."

CHAPTER 7

Estelle Boucher adjusted her scarf, the only color accent to her black pant suit, and not much color at that – a muted red, white, and blue of the French flag, sending its own subminimal message that she was all for France. A lie of course, because she was all for Estelle.

Her slingback heels clacked on the burnished stone stairs leading to the third floor of the elegant headquarters of the Ministry for Europe and Foreign Affairs, one of the seven French national ministries. This was where the work was carried out, along with the deal making and backstabbing.

When she first began to consult there, she felt like a waif in the presence of royalty, but soon she saw through the gentile courtesy. She discovered to her emmense pleasure that these people were cut from the same fabric as Vincent Ballou, leader of the Dockers street gang back at home. Heavy on ego and ambition, light on integrity. She could swim with these fish, as they said on Guadeloupe.

In less than a year, she had ingratiated herself with her boss, Marice Blanchette, and with selected power brokers, and indeed she had made a difference as a mover and shaker. Always for her benefit, and at times even for the benefit of France.

She entered the conference room and made her way to her usual spot at the conference table, next to Maurice, and halfway down from the chair of the group, Charles. He entered, nodded for everyone to sit, and took his place at the head of the table. Conversation stopped and a dozen eyes gazed at the man, dignified and carrying leadership like a mantle, comfortable about his strong shoulders.

As leader of the Inter-ministerial Mission for Combating Drugs and Addictive Behaviors, he murmured his greetings to the attendees from other ministries and their supporting staff. His gaze paused a moment too long on Estelle, and she lowered her eyes and nodded discreetly.

Good – he wants to continue our new relationship as mentor and student. Her gut tightened at thoughts of her goal – an exclusive professional and intimate relationship with the man.

By her side, Maurice fidgeted, no doubt his reaction to that look by Charles, directly at Estelle, threatening the dominance that Maurice thought he held over her. She made a note to declare to Maurice that he was her uncontested superior, because her aim was always to lull him into feeling he held that power. Which enabled her to ferret out the secrets he should have kept, and traded them in the political marketplace. All while he believed she was maintaining workplace and bedroom confidences.

Charles made a final scan of the room, checked that the door was closed, then said, "Thank you all for attending. We have a single topic today – confirmation of our position regarding this afternoon's kick-off meeting with the Mexican delegation for Operation Kingfish. The Mexicans have been coy about details of the operation, claiming security concerns. I did learn that the goals of the operation are to apprehend, try, convict, and imprison Bernardo Cabral. He's a leading drug lord in Mexico, and the source of almost all drugs smuggled into France from that country. I'm sure you've heard about it in the news."

Heads nodded and Charles continued, "One other detail I received from my Mexican counterpart is that Bernard's drug smuggling route is by ocean to Guadeloupe, and from there by air to France." He paused for a moment, then looked at Maurice. "On the subject of this afternoon's Operation Kingfish meeting at the Mexican embassy, I have received an urgent invitation to attend a special ministerial conference at Elysée Palace. I have delegated Maurice to serve as my representative at the embassy meeting."

Maurice nodded smugly and glanced at his archrival across the table, who pressed his lips tight and kept his eyes firmly on Charles.

Charles looked at the man, a senior member from another ministry, and said brightly, "Why don't you begin?"

Estelle saw the man's expression soften at the diplomatic olive branch. He shuffled his notes, awaiting attention to shift to him, and presented his thoughts in his long-winded way. As usual, he peppered his presentation with numerous references to supposed expertise in his ministry that was ripe for application to Operation Kingfish.

Charles had assumed his 'studiously listening' expression of constant eye contact and nods at the appropriate moments. The others, having grown fatigued at the blatant self-serving monologue, displayed less-intent postures.

Estelle was an exception. She listened intently indeed, searching beneath the surface for innuendo, tone, and word choice. As always, she was rewarded with a tidbit or two worthy of trade within her circle of contacts, and in this case, a reference to a specific date related to another sensitive project. She noted the date, not daring to write it down for fear of alerting him or someone else, on their own information-mining expedition.

After Charles pointedly looked at his watch for the second time, the man terminated his presentation. Charles then called on the lead members of the half-dozen organizations represented, and then several of their staff experts. A few people offered new ideas, but mostly they rehashed key points from previous meetings.

Meanwhile, whispered side discussions popped up among members of each organization. Feeling the need to bolster Maurice's ego, Estelle leaned close, keeping her voice low.

"I still feel like an intruder at these gatherings," she said, modestly, playing the part of the loyal student at the feet of her master.

"Why?" he asked. "There are other women, other consultants here."

"But they've been trained on their subjects."

"Ha! You are a quick study to my teaching."

"There is that. But I cannot hold a candle to your amazing insights."

"You are too kind, Estelle."

Estelle drew a contented breath. His ego was pumped up.

"By the way," Maurice said, "are you on for the meeting this afternoon? Charles wouldn't mind if I took you along. Consider it part of your training."

She cocked her head in feigned surprise. "Thank you. I'd love to go, but isn't it by invitation only?"

"True for the meeting, but you are more than welcome at the reception."

"Then yes, I'll go. I want to see who's there. I'm certain to know several from the French side." She grinned. "While you're at the meeting, I'll circulate and learn all the gossip. People love to show off what they know, and the bits and pieces form a bigger picture."

"Especially after drinking a glass of tequila."

"Yes, to loosen the tongue."

As the presentations continued, Estelle carefully gauged each speaker's expressions, and Charles' reaction. She had come to learn that the tiniest quirk of his lips meant approval, and a barely noticeable wrinkle between his eyebrows indicated disapproval. She knew the approved people would receive a nudge toward his inner circle as part of his power plays and empire building within the organization.

The final invited presentations ended and the room became silent. Estelle was one of three attendees not asked to formally present, though at one point she had received eye contact from Charles, and he had asked her a question.

But Maurice interceded with an answer. Charles pretended not to notice Maurice's maneuver, but Estelle caught that wrinkle between Charles' eyes – he was irritated with Maurice, which aligned nicely with Estelle's scheme.

Charles let the contents of the presentations sink in, enabling new thoughts to bubble to the surface of one or more attendees' minds.

A chair creaked.

Clothing rustled as someone changed position in their chair.

Charles' gaze moved from person to person, and when it reached her, she noticed a momentary glint in his eyes. She gave him a private smile and raised her hand – not high – only a few centimeters off the top of the conference table.

His expression instantly returned to all-business. "Yes, Estelle?"

CHAPTER 8

Bleary-eyed in Paris' Charles de Gaulle Airport after the redeye from Guadeloupe, Angela followed Jean through passport control and baggage claim, down several levels, into to a boxy train, through the countryside, into a tunnel, onto the Metro, and at last up a flight of stairs to the open air in the center of Paris

Her first impression was the delightful architecture, so detailed on the facades, entries, and windows. She loved the double-sloped mansard roofs and the iron scrollwork on balconies.

Her next impression was the stench of diesel fumes from buses and trucks. *Ugg.*

Then the hurried big-city crowds, where even the blue jeans-wearing tourists appeared to be intent only on getting to their destinations while ignoring the wonderful sights on the way.

Across from their Jardin des Tuileries Metro stop she spotted the manicured Tuileries Garden. They would have to take a walk there.

Again, the people caught her attention and she said to Jean, quietly, so as not to openly declare they were newbies to the City of Light, "Look how the French women dress and how they walk. They really have a special fashion flair, don't you think?"

"They seem haughty to me."

"Ha, *ma chère*, that's part of the look."

"As if they're walking a runway at a fashion show?"

"No, sweetie." She looked at him. "Now you're teasing me, aren't you?"

He gave her a kiss and grinned. She kissed him back, but only a quick peck, remembering the French were pretty staid when it came to public show of affection.

Then she had a dark thought.

Estelle. Jean's ex-girlfriend.

"Do you think we'll see her?"

Jean frowned. He gestured down the arcaded passage that paralleled the street.

"Our hotel is this way." After a few steps, with their suitcase rollers clacking in time with gaps in the walkway, he added, "Estelle being at the meeting? I'm afraid so, now that I've thought about it. She's tied in with the diplomatic community. The business community as well."

"Would she dress like the women we see here?"

He grinned. "She will be elegant. It's in her genes."

"But she'll have to dress casually, right?"

"Yes, but be prepared."

"What does that mean? Are you nervous about seeing her again?"

"It means she will try to steal the show, to get all the men to look at her."

"Her front or her back?"

"*Mon Dieu*, Angela!"

"Just asking. And you didn't answer my question. Do you feel nervous?"

"Not nervous exactly, because I'm up to her tricks. She'll come on with gushy smiles and compliments, but her eyes will give it away, and her phrasing, designed to make her look and sound better and smarter than any woman present, and most men." He chuckled.

"Do you think she is? Smarter, I mean."

He nodded. "In the arena of manipulation she is a natural. The best I've ever seen."

"Better than the commodore?"

Jean guffawed. "The commodore is at the bottom of the pile for manipulation. He is completely transparent. Estelle is all smoke and mirrors. I usually didn't realize I was manipulated until hours after being with her. She subtly guided me where to eat, who we'd go out with, what we'd wear."

"What you'd wear?"

"Sure. Luckily, I only had a few shirts and trousers and two pairs of shoes. I couldn't afford a big wardrobe, and had no desire for one, in spite of her."

"Jean, I just had a thought. she's probably got half a dozen men wrapped around her little finger."

"No doubt."

"What do you think she wants?"

"Good question. I've wondered the same thing. She seems to want power."

"Power? She doesn't want to be on the cover of a fashion magazine? Or nab a billionaire husband?"

He shrugged. "No, I think it's power."

"But how? In the diplomatic corps?"

"Maybe."

Angela gave this some thought. "I have a funny feeling, Jean. I think she'll have an agenda at the reception. I want to talk with her."

He looked surprised. "To match wits with her?"

"Not blatantly, but I'm curious about how she manipulates people, without giving herself away."

"Careful of her claws," he warned. "She can jump right out of her proper-lady skin and fight dirty."

Angela chuckled. "Thanks. I'll keep my cool. Okay, I'm done talking about Estelle. Let's have fun in Paris."

"It's nearly noon. We need to be at the Mexican embassy by three."

"Let's get lunch – I'll order real French *steak-frites*."

He laughed. "Me too! Tell me, what do you think? Do you like it here so far?"

"Oh Jean, I love Paris! I really don't care about Estelle and her power plans. I care about you and me. This is all wonderful. Though flying was a little scary."

"Ha! What a joke. You sail through killer squalls and never break a sweat."

She poked him in the ribs. "You know what I mean. An airplane is closed in with no wind in your face, and you can't see the waves coming. It's like having a blanket over your head while being helplessly jiggled around."

She paused in front of a shop window. "I see scarves to die for," she said wistfully, then changed to a determined tone. "No –I need to experience Paris. This city has entranced me since I was a little girl. God, Jean, I still can't believe we're really here."

"You do want lunch, right?"

"Oh, yes," she said, unable contain her excitement. "I'm starved. But let's drop off our stuff first."

"Good idea. Our hotel is just another block."

They wheeled their bags past the doorman and entered a quiet, dignified lobby, a sharp contrast to the bustle of the arcade. A desk clerk nodded formally when Jean said they had reservations.

"*Bon jour*, you are most welcome to Paris and to Hotel Jardin des Tuileries. But alas, check-in is later in the day – three o'clock. Of course, I would be pleased to hold your luggage."

Jean frowned. "We have to prepare for a formal affair. Very formal. At three o'clock. Is there a possibility of checking in earlier?"

The desk clerk must have noticed Angela smiling warmly at him, and with what Jean identified as French gallantry, he nodded politely toward her, and in an officious tone said to Jean, "Let me see. Ah yes, we do have a room that will soon be ready. You will go out for a breath of fresh air first perhaps, then return at one thirty? Is that sufficient time?"

"Yes," Jean said, beaming. *"Vous êtes très gentil."*

Leaving their luggage behind, they strode hand-in-hand along the arcade, around Place de la Concorde and its obelisk, and up the broad, tree-lined Champs-Élysées. They window-shopped at elegant stores, with Angela's eye caught by the fashions of Dior and Chanel, and Jean pausing to admire the watches at Tissot.

Coming as an unwelcome surprise, the high-end fashions and even the watches reminded Angela of Estelle. Jean's ex would wear those designer clothes and one of the dazzling jeweled watches.

Was the woman up to something in particular, connected with the meeting? Was that why Jean suspected she would show up at the reception? What sort of power could she gain from the upcoming French-Mexican operation? But Angela's stomach began to growl and she turned her mind to lunch.

They found seats at an outside restaurant only blocks from the upper end of the Champs and its monumental Arc de Triomphe.

Both ordered *steak-frites* and wine and ate silently for several minutes.

Angela gestured toward her half-eaten meal. "It's not as good as mine, but it'll do." She laughed.

Jean grinned. "I agree – yours are the best."

She gazed at passersby. "This feels like a dream, especially because the trip came up so suddenly."

"It does to me, too. Even though I've been here before, I don't remember much, except for the diesel exhaust."

"So here we are, on vacation in June with sunny skies, and only a few hours of business to interfere with our pleasure." She arched her eyebrows. "And no possibility of an emergency call to rush back to LA VIOLETTE to rescue someone at sea."

"No need to hide my phone," he agreed.

She smirked. She'd never actually hidden it, but had often threatened to do so.

Jean checked his watch.

"I think we need to go back and get ready."

"Ok. Let's cross the street to check out the stores on the other side."

With the reception start-time in mind, Jean upped their pace and Angela didn't ask to pause at the glittering showcase windows. She wanted him to shine at the reception and at the meeting, feeling that this could be a professional opportunity, but she certainly did not hope for him to be stationed in France.

Judging by Jean's upbeat mood, she figured he felt the same about Paris as she did. Since they'd arrived, he seemed more relaxed and romantic, hugging her now and then, looking as if he wanted to kiss her but holding back like a Parisian.

She wondered, not for the first time, if he might take this opportunity to propose to her. They'd known each other for only a few months, but they had grown so close, shared so many experiences. Angela's friend Catherine had admonished them to 'get a room' more than once. And later had added that they were certainly a couple, with the same values. 'You guys even finish each other's sentences,' she'd teased.

But to get married? Angela wondered. He was the guy, that was for sure. But did she have more to do, more to see before settling down with a husband and, perhaps, children?

But thoughts of the meeting intruded.

"Jean," she said slowly, "I've been thinking. Doesn't this assignment to fly to Paris under cover as a tourist with your girlfriend, all to attend one short meeting, seem odd to you?"

His expression darkened. "It does. On the surface, it's just an unexplained order from on high. But the commodore mentioned the drug war, and that's important enough for secrecy and unconventional orders. My guess is the meeting is an attempt by France and Mexico to show the commitment of both governments to fight the drug cartels, big time. Though what kind of action will come of it I don't know."

"I guess they think something will happen at sea. Is that why you're invited?"

He nodded. "It's the only reason that makes sense. We know drugs are smuggled to Guadeloupe by sea. That mission this week was to rescue a smuggler with a full load of drugs."

"But you're already looking for smugglers."

"Yep, me and other police on land, and coast guards from other islands."

"Then there must be other reasons for you to be here."

He squeezed her hand. "My gosh, you are the detective. Here I am, just an officer obeying orders, and you're asking these good questions."

She gave him a squeeze back. "Just curious, I guess."

"Well, I agree with you that this operation must be about something larger than the smuggling we've seen up to now. There's got to be another dimension to make both countries go to all this trouble."

She nodded thoughtfully. But it still seemed odd that Jean hadn't been given more specific instructions about his mission to Paris.

In their room, they showered. Angela wrapped herself in the complementary bathrobe, worn alluringly partially opened.

He toweled off and gave her a lecherous look. "I'll bet you're naked as a hummingbird under that robe."

"Ha, wouldn't you like to know, Captain Jean. Too bad."

"Maybe we should test the mattress."

"Mmm. Do we have time?"

"We don't need much."

"Do we have enough?"
He checked his watch. "*Merde*. We don't. Okay, later."
"Too bad." She kissed him.
"I need a cold shower."

CHAPTER 9

Charles had saved Estelle for last so she could listen to all the others' presentations. She had the devious mind to put it all together, matching Operation Kingfish requirements to the goals of his group, and more importantly, his personal goals.

Weeks ago, he had identified her as an ally and considered enlisting her as his protégé. Discrete inquiries revealed she had graduated university with honors and completed a grueling post-graduate year at the Sorbonne. Born and raised in Guadeloupe, she had been a wild young woman, even joining a dangerous urban gang. After a year in a Swiss private school, she came to Paris under the wing of the notorious Sabrina Abon, also of Guadeloupe and also wild.

Mon Dieu, the things Sabrina must have taught her. Or could it be the other way around? Perhaps Estelle had shown Sabrina a trick or two in manipulating people to her own purposes. Both of them were hellcats to be sure, of inestimable value in the cut-throat world of politics and diplomacy. Of value, yes, but only when there was a shared goal. Otherwise, such a person was a menace, to be dealt with harshly.

Charles recognized that Estelle had never attempted to undermine him, though she had done so to others. The reason was simple – she never took on an adversary who was more powerful than herself. Charles felt a second reason she had never tried to undermine him was because she wished to become his ally.

Regarding a mentor-protégé relationship, of high importance was that she understood his priorities. This was a must, so she could properly support him. Thinking back to their mentoring meeting, he recalled that she showed more interest in topics related to his career goals than to her own technical questions.

Several of her supposedly offhand comments revealed she knew how to play the political game. She demonstrated a twillingness to adapt to his needs, knowing he would support her advancement in step with his own. Estelle understood that the mentor-protégé relationship would enable both to gain power.

Charles returned his attention to the present.

With all participants' eyes on Estelle, and her glancing at him for a go-ahead, he smiled encouragingly. She began, her tone confident, her pace measured.

"I did have several thoughts."

Next to her, Maurice fidgeted, no doubt stewing that he should have jumped in and overridden Charles' invitation to her, claiming his authority as the senior member of their duo. Charles scowled at Maurice and the man stilled, understanding the warning.

Estelle summarized key positions she knew Charles held, and discredited positions he didn't approve of, all her points reinforced with sound reasoning. Her logic was couched in terms of how his group's actions would contribute to the success of Operation Kingfish. Twice, she added a point that bridged and strengthened separate elements. She even aligned her presentation to exclude an initial error he had made, in which two elements included contradictory points.

She continued, "In what follows, my final point, I will cover new ground, so feel free to interrupt with comments and questions. First, a question of my own: Where does our group, the Inter-ministerial Mission for Combating Drugs and Addictive Behaviors, fit into Operation Kingfish? More specifically, how can we best contribute to achieving the four goals of apprehending, trying, convicting, and imprisoning Bernardo Cabral? The answer is clearly that our contribution must be to support the 'apprehending' phase."

A man asked, "But Estelle, aren't the Mexican police and other agencies quite capable of carrying out apprehensions in their own country?"

"Yes, they are – inside Mexico. But not if Cabral escapes the police, bypasses customs, and eludes any other official enforcement units within the country."

The man frowned. "But they'll certainly guard all air and sea terminals. I think they'll put a tight lid on the country for this guy."

"I agree. But there are limits. Can they shut down every beach where he could be picked up by a fast boat? Do they search every sportfish in every marina? Or guard all the disused and private airstrips where a plane could be stationed for a get-away?"

The man nodded, a thoughtful look on his face.

A woman asked, "But it seems this is a moot point. The police have his house surrounded, don't they?"

"Yes, his villa in Mexico City, which they are likely prepared to storm. But what if he has an escape route to get outside the police cordon?"

"So," the woman said, "you think he'll escape from his villa?"

"Not exactly. I'm saying that the best way we can assist the operation is to be ready to apprehend him if he escapes the police and other Mexican enforcement services and flees the country."

"Jeeze, what are the chances of that?" asked another man.

"I don't have a number for you. I will say that it's happened often enough in the past, including high-security prison escapes, and escape by tunnel."

Charles said, "I think Estelle has a good point. We have to ensure we remain within our charter and within our combined expertise. Estelle, please continue, and I would like to hear specifics. After all, Cabral has multiple choices of destination, route, and mode of transport. Where do you suggest we focus our resources?"

"I think we must examine the problem from his point of view. He was born and raised in Mexico, so I believe he would opt for a country of refuge in Europe, where the culture and perhaps even the language, are familiar to him.

"As far as his route, the shortest one possible is what he will likely choose. He will also seek to minimize the duration of his exposure between departing his villa and arriving at a safe destination. Ideally, the entire escape will occur during a period in which the police believe he is still inside his villa, surrounded."

"A flight across the Atlantic?" the woman said in a disbelieving tone. "That sounds far-fetched to me."

"I agree," Estelle responded. "I believe he will stop along the way and switch modes of transport to better elude the police in case they discover he has escaped their cordon." She gave her listeners only a moment to ponder that thought, then said, "An ideal place would be Guadeloupe."

"The French island? Why?"

"Because he passes his drugs through Guadeloupe on their way to France and other European countries. He knows and trusts the people he works with there."

The woman seemed unconvinced. "He'd trust them?"

Estelle looked her in the eye. "He is their customer and their boss. If they help him, they strengthen a bond, if they double cross him, they and their families will be murdered by his enforcers. Besides, they've worked together to smuggle drugs under our collective noses for years. They will view smuggling a single person as fairly easy."

"Where would he go in Europe?" another man asked.

"Several countries come to mind. One is Switzerland. Another is Spain."

Charles reflected on Estelle's logic – Cabral escaping Mexico, fleeing to Guadeloupe, then on to Europe. Certainly, the most dangerous part of the journey would be exposure during the transfer in Guadeloupe. There, he would be most vulnerable, especially if his absence had been discovered.

"Thank you, all," Estelle said, and turned to Charles.

He surveyed the attendees, evaluating expressions of agreement, of doubt, of anger. The anger was the most dangerous, evident in the eyes of the first man to question Estelle.

He was from the Ministry of Justice and had argued for assisting the Mexicans in developing their legal case against Cabral. It was a bad idea. Hell, he and his staff didn't even speak their language.

The man had pointed out that Mexico and France shared Napoleonic Law as the basis for their legal systems. But at the detailed level, where trials were won or lost, the systems and processes varied greatly between France and Mexico. The man had argued his point strongly in the past, and even though Charles had been clear that he did not agree, here he was again pushing for a major role in the operation. Charles decided he must remain vigilant in the coming days for possible political backlash from the man.

Maurice gained Charles' attention and repeated Estelle's key points, bathing in the light of her presentation as if it were his. Charles pretended not to notice the cheap gambit and wondered when Estelle would disassociate herself from Maurice. From her frown, the time appeared near.

Charles addressed the group. "We are all aware from our previous meetings that Guadeloupe is key to Cabral's drug smuggling operation. I have recently participated in very high-level discussions about this."

He made eye contact with the recalcitrant man, making sure he realized that he, Charles, was referring to the Council of Ministers, directly under the prime minister, and that it would thus be wise for the man to refrain from rocking the boat.

Charles continued, "I have been authorized to share details of Operation Kingfish with the Maritime Gendarmerie on Guadeloupe, and toward that end I have invited the captain of their armed patrol boat to attend this afternoon's meeting with the Mexican delegation."

He turned to Maurice. "All delegates to that meeting will be in civilian attire, though there will be people there who will recognize faces and the word will filter out. Maurice, you will not approach this man. His name is Jean Aguillard. He is an unknown in Paris, and I wish for that to remain the case."

"Yes, Charles."

Charles leaned back in his chair taking a cautious breath of victory but sat upright when he spotted the blush on Estelle's cheeks, no doubt brought on by the mention of Jean Aguillard. Charles' gut lurched. Her familiarity with the gangs, and now with the Maritime Gendarmerie officer, were muddling the stew, presenting too many opportunities for her to stray from his priorities in favor of her own.

He was suddenly impatient to wrap that woman up tight in allegiance to him, make her realize her days as a free-wheeling independent consultant were over. He would tolerate no leaks of information and would insist on knowing all her activities.

Her loyalty to him was paramont, and the price of betrayal dire. All this he planned to make explicitly clear at their next meeting.

CHAPTER 10

Angela held hands with Jean in the backseat of the zooming taxi, threading its way down Rue de Rivoli, left at Place de la Concorde, and, surprisingly, across the Seine. She admired the art nouveau lamps on the bridge but was puzzled to be crossing the river.

Jean leaned forward and asked the driver, "Isn't the Mexican Embassy on the same side of the river as our hotel?"

Over his shoulder the driver declared, "*Ah oui, c'est vrai*, you are right, but this route is *plus rapide*."

At the end of the bridge, he sped through a traffic light as it changed from yellow to red, then careened right, onto a road paralleling the river.

Angela, disappointed at not catching glimpses of elegant shops, asked, "So this is faster than taking Champs-Élysées?"

His voice became diffident. "Oh, definitely, *madame*. You are in a hurry, *n'est-ce pas? Nous arrivons* in only twelve minutes from your hotel."

He sped onto another bridge back across the river and wound through elegant apartment neighborhoods, and finally stopped in front of the Mexican Embassy.

He turned and quoted the charge from the meter and smiled, collecting his payment. "You see, a fast trip. Thank you, *madame et monsieur. Bonne journée*."

On the sidewalk in front of the embassy, Jean said, "Do our taxis drive like that?"

She grinned. "No, but I do on my TaoTao street scooter."

He shrugged. "I guess I do as well, when I'm on a mission to visit you in your home. Anyway, here we are."

Angela linked her arm with his, and checked out the half dozen others entering the double doors to the rather plain-faced, four-story tan structure. A Mexican flag flew high on the building, and above the entrance was a painting of the eagle-and-snake seal of Mexico, in a style that looked like Art Déco.

She and Jean joined a steady stream of guests entering the embassy. Inside, she accepted a flute of Champagne from a white-jacketed attendant and admired the spacious atrium, definitely Art Déco, 'functional with flair,' with flat beige walls, geometrical ironwork railings on stairs, understated lighting fixtures, and open balconies.

To one side a trio of musicians played a gentle classical piece, and a small bar provided drinks, including wine and three brands of tequila. She opted for wine, and Jean asked for soda water. She knew he could hold his booze, but also remembered he was officially on duty.

Jean guided her to the edge of the crowd, now pairing and clumping into discussion groups, filling the room with French and Spanish conversation. There were no uniforms, except for the circulating attendants, now offering Mexican *tapas* and French *hors d'oeuvres*. She tried a colorful *tapa*, munched, found it too spicy, and switched to a French morsel, pairing nicely with her Chardonnay.

A couple of late arrivals entered, rounding out the number of guests to about forty. All were nicely dressed, stylish and modestly jeweled, fitting the dress code. She felt okay but not so special in her knee-length tailored black skirt, medium-height heels, and French-blue blouse, all topped off with a blue and red scarf she'd borrowed from Catherine.

She wished she'd styled her hair, but oh well – she'd washed her hair in the shower, blow-dried, and wore it as usual with a slight curl, just touching her shoulders. Plus lipstick and a bit of makeup.

She smiled to herself when she noticed men checking her out, knowing that her skirt, if not her blouse, did show off her slim figure. But she found herself nervous in a room full of strangers and at a level of formality rarely experienced on Guadeloupe. She was thankful to have Jean there – to be alone would be even more uncomfortable.

She asked him, "Do you see anyone you recognize, maybe from their photo?"

"Not a soul," he murmured. "Frankly, I'd rather be on the flying bridge of LA VIOLETTE."

"Me too, on SECOND WIND at sea.

"Oh, I almost forgot. I've got to visit the head of the Maritime Gendarmerie at headquarters after this meeting."

"In Paris?"

"Yes, just a twenty-minute ride from here. It's a courtesy call. Won't take long."

"And you'll make a new contact. I'm sure you'll make a great impression, Jean. Maybe you'll get more exciting missions in the future. Like to Rome or England."

He chuckled. "Maybe. The travel would be fun, but not the politics."

"But you're very experienced. You would contribute with practical suggestions when discussions wandered into theory, don't you think?" He didn't answer, and she added in a mischievous tone, "My gosh, you are world class at rescuing a young woman from the clutches of pirates."

He gave her a discrete squeeze. "Thanks."

An attendant apprpoached Jean and asked in passable French, "You are Lieutenant Aguillard, sir?"

"Yes."

"The meeting is about to begin." He gestured to a stairway. "The room is on the second level. You will see the door. Please show your military ID to the sentry."

"Very well. Thank you."

The man moved on, glanced at a piece of paper in his hand, scanned the crowd, and aimed toward, Angela assumed, the next invitee."

"Time to go," Jean said.

"You look so handsome."

"Thanks. You are the prettiest woman here."

"I guess we can't kiss."

"No, that would be *gauche*."

She squeezed his hand. "*Bon chance*."

"Merci, ma chère."

And he was off, winding through the crowd and up the stairs. Angela drew a breath, girding herself to remain calm in the coming days after they returned home, when he could face danger at sea because of his role in whatever this Frensh-Mexican project was all about.

She wanted him safe and alive.

Which brought to mind her own goal, to gather information that might help him carry out his duties, and also to learn about what Estelle might be up to, which might or might not involve the project. She decided to start immediately, talking with others left out of the meeting, gathering bits of gossip here and a bit there, and perhaps making connections.

She admitted that the Estelle challenge was uppermost in her mind, mostly to keep that woman from trying to snatch Jean away from her, but she also had a strange feeling the woman was up to something more than romantic intrigue.

Angela examined the crowd, trying to identify Estelle, whom she'd never seen before. She counted three young women who seemed to fit the bill. One raven-haired beauty was close-by and spoke quietly, but loud enough for Angela to discern that her language was Spanish. The other two women carried themselves with poise and appeared to be in their mid-twenties, but she wasn't close enough to hear their conversation.

Angela let her eyes roam among the rest of the crowd, though often returning to the two women to gain more insight. The first one's dress appeared to be exquisitely designed, totally complimenting her figure.

The dress appeared to be a part of herself, creating a continuity of her body's energy and allure. As she gestured dramatically, the fabric swayed from the motion of her shoulders and hips. The second woman's dress lacked that feeling of one-ness with her, and her gestures were confined to hands and a refined lift of the arm, all projecting a self-contained nature. But she had an intellectual intensity lacking in the first woman, and a certain strength in her expressions.

Angela concluded that either woman could be Estelle. One was dramatic, the other self-contained. Or, Estelle could be another woman at the reception.

Angela shrugged – she'd gained as much from casual observation as possible, and didn't want to walk up to a stranger and ask if she was the witch that Jean talked about. She'd give thought to a likely reason to start a conversation and then introduce herself.

She wondered if Jean had ever mentioned her to Estelle. Probably, but certainly only the barest of details. The man was discrete, and loyalty was his middle name.

But this was getting her nowhere. She needed to circulate, try to join a discussion. She wound through the throng and noticed that, with almost half the original crowd now in their meeting, the floor had cleared considerably. The remaining guests were joining new partners, sometimes forming groups. Angela spotted one person standing at the edge of the crowd, half-filled wine glass in hand.

Angela meandered toward the woman, who wore an expensive-looking with a scarf around her neck, hopefully a sign that she was French. Which better be the case, because Angela spoke very little Spanish. As she grew near, the woman waved and greeted another woman. She spoke French, but now engaged in a dialogue that revealed they were close friends and likely not open to a stranger joining in.

Momentarily at a loss, Angela ran her eyes beyond the crowd, past front door, bar, and the musical trio, to a hallway that led further back into the building. Probably to offices. And rest rooms.

An idea sprang to mind.

Risky, but with a chance of gaining plenty of information about the purpose of the meeting and details about the mission itself.

She entered the hallway. After only a few meters, she was rewarded with two Art Déco signs – *'Mujeres'* and *'Hombres.'*

She ducked into the former, entering a tiled ladies' room with four stalls and two wide sinks. All Art Déco, of course. She noticed that the sinks were mounted on cabinets, and a quick check confirmed the cabinets were only half full, containing spare paper towels, toilet paper, and tissues.

Angela pushed open the doors of all the stalls, confirmed she was alone, and locked herself in the stall farthest from the door, closest to a half-open window to the outside. She quickly undressed and folded her clothes into a compact bundle. Rushed out and placed her clothes and shoes inside a cabinet, hidden behind the supplies, and nipped back to the stall and locked the door.

She shape-shifted to her black cat form and stood on the cool tile of floor. Looking under the gap in the stall siding, she confirmed she was still alone.

Approaching female voices sounded from the hallway, and Angela urgently scampered under the gap in the stall, leaped onto a radiator, bounded up the windowsill, and out through the window. She landed in a small courtyard, open to the sky, and bordered by the walls of the embassy and adjacent buildings. On the embassy wall were four first-floor windows, including those of the restrooms, and a closed door.

Cooking smells wafted from the right-hand window. She jumped onto a pile of wooden boxes, to the sill and into a hot kitchen, where people speaking Spanish and French fussed over trays of snacks. She bounded onto the floor and ran out a swinging service door as an attendant departed, a tray of tapas balanced on his right hand.

Remaining close to the wall, she followed the attendant to the atrium, then scurried up the stairs to the second story. She noticed an open door through which several people passed, pausing for ID check by a stern-faced uniformed guard.

Obviously, the meeting room.

The next delegate stepped to the door and displayed her ID to the guard. The two exchanged greetings in Spanish and Angela made her move, dashing behind the guard, through the entrance, and into the room.

The dominant feature of the room was a burnished wooden conference table. Beyond that stood a white presentation screen. In in the space between the door and the table men and women chatted in groups. The tone of discussion was serious, and as expected, in French and Spanish. Luckily no one had found a common single language, like English. Good for her, because she spoke little of that language, or any other, except a bit of the calypso-accented Caribbean Creole.

She spied Jean with a man and woman, the three of them in somber discussion. God, he was so handsome and charming. She loved him to pieces; he had become a huge part of her life. She wondered about marriage, but forced herself to refocus on her reason for being there.

She searched for likely delegates to spy on, especially those positioned close to the extra chairs lined up against the wall, under which she could hide. She found a group of people three meters from her position beside the entrance and made her way there and crouched under a chair. She listened, pleased to hear their language was French.

One man seemed to be holding the attention of the other four or five people in the circle. He was thin, looking like a university professor, and his words were technical, delivered in a monotone. But the others leaned close, so she tuned in.

Unfortunately, the sound of multiple conversations in two languages drowned out all but the odd phrase from the thin man. She caught 'capture,' 'police cordon,' 'Operation Kingfish,' and 'Mexican drug lord.' There was no mention of why the French were involved.

Off to her right, very near, someone sneezed, then again, and just as she wondered whether to be concerned, she felt a woman reach beneath her chair and snatch her, lifting her high, and remarking that her partner at the meeting was deathly allergic to cats. At least, that was what Angela gathered, for the woman spoke in agitated Spanish.

The woman marched out of the room, high heels clacking angrily on the marble floor, and dropped Angela at the sentry's feet, spurting what sounded like angry phrases about cats. The sentry scowled and bent to seize Angela, but she lunged for the stairs, praying that the swinging door to the kitchen would be open.

CHAPTER 11

Jean turned toward a disruption at the entrance to the meeting room and spotted a member of the Mexican delegation entering, brushing her hands. The man next to him murmured, “She just threw out a cat.”

“A cat?”

“Yeah, her associate is allergic to cats. I guess it was on the hunt, in case one of the tapa sardines fell to the floor.”

Jean shook his head. A mad taxi ride. A cat. He wondered what was next. He thought of Angela, alone one story below, and wished he’d known someone there he could have introduced her to, so she had company.

God, he loved her. Hmm. He knew he wanted to marry this wonderful woman and he believed she would say yes. Propose under the Eiffel Tower? Maybe. Food for thought.

He surveyed the men and women in the room, mostly senior with urbane manners, but peppered among them were four early-forties, very fit, granite-faced men – two French and two Mexican. Their posture and short hair branded them as police or military. Jean was tempted to join their group, but they seemed intent on their privacy, huddled close and occasionally glancing over their shoulders, as if the information they shared among themselves was to be jealously guarded.

A distinguished man took his place at the head of the conference table and pulled out his chair. Conversation dwindled and the Mexican delegation, with the French following suit, made their way to seats on either side of the table. Jean noticed a tented name card at each place. He found his toward the bottom of the table and sat. Several staff sat in chairs lined up along the wall, behind their respective delegates at the table. There were muted introductions and handshakes across the table as French and Mexican delegates identified their counterparts.

The man at the head of the table called the meeting to order in passable French, which he then repeated in Spanish.

"I welcome you all here to our organizational meeting of Operation Kingfish. Thank you for attending, whether flying from Mexico or, I understand, the southern island of Guadeloupe. Who is here from that island please?"

Jean, feeling his face flush at the unexpected attention, raised his hand slightly.

The man smiled. "*Bienvenue à Paris.* I hope you find the weather agreeable and the city entertaining, even though there are no pretty beaches."

Jean nodded, wondering for the tenth time what his role was. Everyone else dutifully chuckled at the man's humor.

Having gained the group's attention, the leader's tone turned somber. "Ladies and gentlemen, we are here on a most serious matter. Briefly put – to arrest, convict, and imprison the Mexican drug lord, Bernardo Cabral."

He paused to allow all present to absorb the operation's previously secret purpose, then said, "Cabral is the major illegal drug supplier from Mexico to France, and his enterprise has worsened an already grave situation. His removal will terminate his operation and will stand as a warning to others that our two nations are absolutely committed to stoping drug production and smuggling."

Jean mentally nodded. Drugs. The bane of Guadeloupe, and France as well. But what was the connection between Mexico and France – and Guadeloupe? Certainly not just that drug boat he'd apprehended two days back. He listened more closely, seeking hints of his role, and growing impatient at the meeting appearing to morph into a bureaucratic organizational discussion.

At length, the leader said, "We are dividing our operational tasks among three working groups. The groups are already separately active, and following our meeting today, they will join in a coordinated fashion. The first group has the delicate goal of minimizing Cabral's influence lurking within our respective governments."

Jean figured that meant getting rid of bribable officials, a number of which must surely be in Cabral's pocket if they warranted the attendion of a separate group.

"The second group is developing our legal plan, beginning with the charging document and continuing with the strategy for prosecution during trial. The group has gathered an unassailable body of evidence to ensure the judge will deny bail, the jury will convict Cabral, and the judge will sentence him to prison for many years. The work of this group is just beginning, and their progress will be reported in due time.

Jean tapped his finger on the table, then quickly stopped when he realized he was blatently showing imppatience. He wondered what Angela was up to. Sipping wine, he guessed.

The leader continued, "We now turn to the third group, a task force from the Guardia Nacional, the Mexican national police. I will turn the floor over to their leader, Colonel Juan Rodriguez."

He gestured to a stone-faced, bulky man sitting to his right at the head of the table, who rose and strode to the screen at the front of the room. He wore civilian attire but had 'police' written all over him, from his ramrod posture to his pugnacious eyes.

Rodriguez gestured to the viewgraph display screen, which bore a logo with the words, 'Guardia Nacional – Justicia y Paz,' and displayed in its center the Mexican national symbol of an eagle devouring a snake.

"Justice and peace," he said in an ironic tone. "In this case, bringing the drug lord Bernardo Cabral to justice in order to improve the peace in our two countries."

He paused for translation to French, then advanced to a slide of a luxurious villa in the Mexican hacienda style, with a courtyard and fountain in its center. Outside the villa ranged a small forest of trees and flowering plants, surrounded by a four-meter high stone wall.

It looked to Jean like a fortress.

Rodriguez quirked his lips, glanced at the four police sitting against the wall, and said in an aggressive tone, "You see where Cabral now resides. A secure base, for sure. But the walls keep him in his place as well, instead of wandering our streets in his armored limosine. Rest assured that we have the means to intrude and arrest this man."

Rodriguez wrapped up with several details and asked if there were any questions.

Jean remained clueless regarding his role. Would he be working with the Guardia Nacional?

The meeting leader asked Rodriguez, "What if Cabral evades capture and escapes Mexico? Will you request international assistance?"

"He will not evade capture. My task force is completely aware of every square meter inside the villa wall, every door and window of the place. We have practiced forced entry with a mock-up. We have an armored vehicle capable of breaching the gate." He waited a beat for other questions, and having none, he resumed his place.

The leader leaned close to Rodriguez and whispered. Rodriguez scowled and shook his head. The leader nodded, as if attempting to defuse an argument, and viewed the attendees, regaining their attention.

"Colonel Rodriquez and I have agreed to disagree on the possibility of Cabral escaping Mexico. I do believe that his chances are nearly nonexistant."

Rodriguez looked down at his firmly clasped hands, his face red.

Jean wondered why the leader was now glancing at him, then away.

"To condinue," the leader said, his voice stern, "we must plan for contingencies. In particular, escape outside of Mexico. We must consider events out of the ordinary, such a terrible storm, an earthquake, a fire, or perhaps a distraction such as an attack on an important person, requiring the immediate response of the task foce assigned to capture Cabral.

"With the possibility of escape in mind, we have looked at Cabral's options – air, land, or sea. North to the United States, south to Latin America, West to the Caribbean and Europe..."

Again the eye contact with Jean.

"...or east to Asia," the leader said. "No matter what the route, he will desire to maintain control at all times. Control. It is of monumental importance to this man, for business success and for survival in his treacherous world. So, let us consider the one route over which he has remarkable control – his drug transmission path from Mexico to France..."

Jean took in a quick breath, beginning to connect the dots. Remembering the burning smugglers' boat two days previously.

"...through the French island of Guadeloupe." Now he stared at Jean and asked, "Who on Guadeloupe is his contact?"

Jean was momentarily taken off balance. How the hell should he know? That was a matter for the *gendarmerie* on shore. Of course, everyone *did* know, and he responded, "The Dockers gang, operating in Pointe-à-Pitre."

The leader smiled in victory. "Led by who?"

"His name is Vicent Ballou."

"And why is he not surrounded as is Cabral?"

Jean felt his temper rise at the man's pugnacious line of questioning, completely out of Jean's area of responsibility. But again, he knew the answer.

"Insufficient evidence. We know the drugs arrive, we know most depart and some remain to tarnish lives on our island."

"Exactly."

No apology to Jean for putting him on the hot seat. What a prick. A glance at Rodriguez showed he shared Jean's feelings.

The leader, gloating, announced, "Again – exactly! It is well known that drugs leave Mexico, pass through Guadeloupe, and, mostly, arrive in France. But the details of the process are not known. I give to you this proof that Cabral has the ideal escape route – known to him, controlled by him, and safe for him."

Rodriguez shook his head.

Jean knew his assignment – intercept a vicious drug lord on the high seas, likely at night in a high-speed boat, constructed of wood or fiberglass for lower radar detection. Protected by a hardened crew, armed with automatic weapons and probably rocket-propelled grenades that are capable of sinking LA VIOLETTE.

The leader went on to describe the organizational details of Operational Kingfish, and talked through a parade of viewgraphs. Buzzwords and acronyms abounded, as a well as lines of authority and responsibility.

Jean paid no attention, his mind contemplating all that could go wrong with his assigned mission, and the little that was under his control.

When the presentation finally ground to a halt, the leader asked if there were any questions.

A man raised his hand. "When do you think Cabral will be arrested?"

The leader glanced only a moment at the brooding Colonel Rodriguez, then said, "Within one week."

Jean, with every nerve in his body tingling in anger, was tempted to raise his hand and ask the leader, "Could you please back up your goal of intercepting Cabral at sea by providing me with four more patrol boats assigned to me for the duration?"

But he knew the answer.

And the consequences of asking the question.

CHAPTER 12

Angela had just slipped her shoes on when she heard the door to the ladies' room open. A woman entered and claimed the stall next to hers. Angela exited her stall, washed hands, and departed the ladies' room, turning toward the atrium.

She paused at the end of the hallway, surveying the crowd and thinking of ways to initiate conversation with the two possible 'Estelles.' She chose an innocent opening line of, 'I wonder when they'll all return.' If the woman spoke French, Angela would engage, and if it was Spanish, Angela would move on after pleasantries, and try the other 'Estelle.'

Angela hoped that the real Estelle would be curious about who Jean had chosen as his plus-one for the trip and reveal her own identity as Jean's friend. *Mon Dieu,* the process felt as though they were rival detectives feeling each other out as possible adversaries.

Women were supposed to be experts at such interrogations but Angela admitted she'd always been more interested in sailing and the sea than the intricacies of human relationships. Her friendships were straight forward, unburdened by social agendas.

She shifted her weight, and a woman standing nearby said, "A chair in a nice café would do well, don't you think?"

Angela smiled at the middle-aged lady. "Yes, my feet are a bit tired, and the wine..."

"It sneaks up on you. Well, the wine, tequila, and *hors d'oeuvres* are fun. The Mexicans are good hosts, don't you think?"

"I agree, and I love the décor."

"Attention to detail. Did you get an opportunity to visit the ladies' room?"

Angela chuckled. "With their Art Déco sinks?"

"Right. Even the signs on the doors. Hmm, if you don't mind my saying, you have an accent from abroad. Are you from the islands?"

"Yes, the British island of St. Lucia in the Caribbean. But now I'm living on Guadeloupe. My French is still a work in progress, I'm afraid."

The woman's eyebrows rose in curiousity, and Angela continued, "I know, you must be asking yourself why would my escort, who is the captain of the Maritime Gendarmerie patrol boat in Guadeloupe, be invited to the meeting they're having upstairs?"

"You are quite correct. My exact thoughts." She grinned mischievously. "My husband is a diplomat and must keep his secrets from me or he will find himself in serious trouble. I am a scientist, and am naturally curious, so I ask myself what is your gallant husband's role in whatever it is the French and Mexicans are planning?"

"As to his role, I haven't a clue, other than I assume he will provide support at sea. On the other hand, I observed four very dour men among those who went upstairs. That could be a clue."

"They're police. You could tell from their haircuts."

"Military style, but I believe they are police."

"Yes, I agree – police. Do you play this game with your husband as well?"

"Not until this trip. His missions have always been to rescue people at sea and to intercept smugglers, and he's open about the details. But he isn't even allowed to tell me the name of this operation, or whatever it is."

"A pity. Sometimes the name is a clue." She glanced around the room. "You'd be surprised how much you can learn at these receptions. Partners – husbands and wives and friends – of the diplomats and their staff each end up picking up a little of what they should not know."

"I understand, and I hope to learn bits from people I talk with."

"Like me?"

"Oh yes." Angela smiled like a conspirator. "And remember, it was you who made your look of curiosity."

"And then you responded. Yes, that is the first rule of the game we play – share information. Give a little and take a little."

"Then I have a little to share with you," Angela murmured, thinking to tell this woman, however friendly, only a portion of what she learned. "I have, er, overheard the word 'capture.' Who or what, I haven't a clue. The word was spoken in a noisy room, so I was not able to determine its context."

The woman gasped. "My God! That's a whole evening's worth of information. It dovetails right into what I learned a few minutes ago. It's the name of a Mexican drug lord – Bernardo Cabral."

"I've heard of him. He murdered his brother to become the cartel leader. He tortures and kills, and is very good at business."

"Yes, very much the success story. He must be the target for the French and Mexican team at the meeting upstairs."

Angela wondered what to ask next, but 'Estelle' number one appeared at her shoulder, frowning at the woman Angela was talking with.

Estelle said to Angela, "*Bonjour mademoiselle.* I believe I know you, at least from your escort when you arrived."

Catching her breath at the surprise appearance, Angela extended her hand. "*Bonjour.* I am Angela Spencer."

"As I thought. *Enchanté, mademoiselle.* I am Estelle Boucher."

They shook, and Estelle again frowned at the other woman, who graciously said to Angela, "I see that you and your friend have things to talk about. Thank you for your company. You have saved me from a boor who has, fortunately, found someone else to entertain, so I am free to hunt." She touched Angela's shoulder and melded into the crowd.

Leaving Angela alone with Estelle Boucher.

For the blink of an eye, Angela glimpsed Estelle's aura, dark gray as a fog, the same as that of an evil person she had known on her home island of St. Lucia. A sneak and a thief.

With the crowd's continuing conversation surrounding them, Estelle scanned Angela with probing intensity. Angela felt as if she were undressing her, literally, and she shivered at the disquieting thought.

Merde. The woman was even more elegant and self-assured than she had appeared from afar. And definitely driven.

To break the silence, Angela said, “I’m happy to meet you in person, Estelle.”

“And I as well. Jean has spoken of you, though briefly and with very little detail in spite of my probing. You are a sailor, correct?”

“I sail, and I have helped protect endangered sea turtles on our island.”

Estelle gestured with a dismissive turn of the wrist. “Oh, Guadeloupe is not *our* island, to be sure. I have left that part of my life resolutely behind.”

“You’ve never returned to Guadeloupe, not even for a short visit?” Angela asked in an innocent voice, letting Estelle guess whether she knew about the trying circumstances of the woman’s departure, and her relationship with a gang member.

Estelle answered, too quickly, “No, I have not returned.”

“But the way you say it – might you return in the future?”

Estelle stared at Angela. “There is always the possibility I suppose.”

Angela was certain the verbal exchange contained a clue, because the emotion in Estelle’s voice was obvious. Guadeloupe was a hot button for the woman, even after several years’ absence. It could be her sadness at not seeing family and friends. Perhaps, but Angela thought it more likely the island was a part of some scheme Estelle was cooking up. Likely, she envisioned a visit, and a plan to stir a pot.

Good grief – the woman’s scheme could involve Operation Kingfish. Angela found herself at a loss for how to proceed.

Estelle changed the subject, obviously to take the spotlight away from herself, remarking in a condescending voice, “Your accent is lovely. I am sure Jean finds it enchanting.”

Angela figured two could change subjects and she responded brightly, “I hope you are enjoying living in Paris. It is such an exciting city.”

Estelle pasted on a smile. “I am firmly ensconced in Paris. It is a civilized place full of wit and progress. I’ve finished my post-graduate classes and accepted a position as a diplomatic consultant.”

She said ‘diplomatic consultant’ as if it were ‘President of France.’

Estelle probed, "I imagine Jean has shared little of the reason he is here. He can be so secretive when he wants to be."

"Yes, he has kept quiet about the meeting."

"Or who was to attend?"

"Well, no. Nothing."

Which was the exact moment Angela noticed a button was missing on Estelle's dress, the fault partially hidden by a fold in the material. The fabric had shifted as Estelle continued to probe, giving nothing away about her own feelings for Jean – past, present, or future.

The missing button was something that should not have mattered at all to Angela, but her mind refused to ignore the anomaly in an otherwise impeccable fashion statement.

The button could have fallen off on the way to the reception or during the past few minutes. But no, Angela now discovered, during another of the woman's broad gestrures, that the button was not lost after all, but safe and secure, beneath the button hole.

An unbuttoned dress.

As the scientist woman would say, 'attention to detail.'

Estelle's outfit, her manner, were sublime. Did a missed button signify anything of importance about the woman? The voice in Angela's mind said 'yes.' To miss an important detail in one sphere of life could lead one to expect the same in another sphere. Like the scheme she might be hatching.

Bringing herself back to the present, Angela became aware of Estelle winding down on her self-aggrandizing monologue, and remarking, "Well, I see the doors to the meeting room have opened and everyone is returning."

Angela nodded and surveyed the descending group of delegates. Some appeared relieved, others in deep thought. There was no sign of Jean. She moved to one side, noticing Estelle maneuver slightly out of her line of sight. Still no Jean.

She felt a sharp bump against her shoulder and heard the clatter of broken glass on the floor.

"My goodness!" Estelle said in a surprised voice.

She glared at a waiter, who was regaining control of his wobbling tray of Champagne flutes and looked daggers back at her.

With his tray back under control, he turned to Angela and said, "I am so sorry, *mademoiselle*. I have spilled Champagne on you."

Angela dabbed at the spill on her shoulder and smiled, "It's okay, *monsieur*. No harm done."

He nodded and moved toward the kitchen. Another waiter arrived and tended to the spill and broken glass on the floor.

Estelle examined the dark blot on Angela's blouse and declared in a syrupy voice. "What a shame. You must sponge this off in the ladies' room. I will be sure to inform Jean."

Off balance from the spill, and angered at the presumptive attitude of Estelle, Angela took a final glance at the stairs but didn't see Jean.

A voice in her head whispered that Estelle had jostled the Champagne tray. Angela could guess why – so Estelle could tell Jean her side of their meeting.

Angela gave her adversary a level look. "Well, Estelle, I'm happy to have met you and wish you all the best on your new position."

The woman's eyes flashed, as if she were dissecting Angela's parting words for double *entendre*. But there was none. Or was there – the word 'position' could have sexual connotations.

CHAPTER 13

Estelle watched the little tart retreat, figuring she'd be out of her hair for a good ten minutes. Glancing up the stairs to the landing, she spotted Maurice and breathed a sigh of relief. The man was lecturing another delegate in his typical academic manner. Great – he'd remain fully distracted for at least ten minutes as well.

Satisfied she had time for a *tête à tête* with Jean, she closely scanned the delegates as they streamed out of the conference room and onto the stairs. There he was, alone and already half way down, searching the crowd, no doubt for his precious Angela.

Too bad, my dear captain, your playmate is presently out of action.

Estelle wound through the swelling crowd toward the stairs, catching a brief view of him as he approached. She wondered how he would greet her. They had not communicated for several weeks, and before that, their exchanges had become less frequent and more emotionally distant.

She must rekindle a bit of the flame.

Estelle chewed her lip, then grinned wolfishly – *perhaps rekindle more than just a bit of the flame.* A roll in the hay would do wonders for their relationship. And her ego.

Jean stepped off the stairs and she glided across the remaining few meters to his side. "Oh, hi, Jean. I thought I saw you."

He turned, his expression momentarily puzzled, then showing recognition, eyes wary, lips closed. She smiled and touched his shoulder, beaming friendship, and his expression softened. He responded in kind, they cheek-kissed, like long-time acquaintances – air kisses only. Too formal for her, but it was a start.

She took his arm and guided him to the edge of the surging throng. Safely ensconced, she began with the 'other woman,' hoping to elicit guilt or doubt on his part to weaken his defenses against her main thrust.

"I met Angela. She was alone and wandering about, poor thing. I introduced myself, to show her a friendly face in the crowd."

He was watchful, his eyes scanning her face, which was something he normally did not do. He had changed for the worse, becoming stubborn. Maybe his position as captain of the patrol boat had gone to his head.

She smiled and continued, "She is such a sweet girl. Imagine, never having travelled beyond the Caribbean islands! Ah, well, I'm sure she'll be able to pick up our manners."

"Guadeloupe is part of France. Our manners are the same."

"My gosh, Jean, not to make a big deal out of it, but there is a difference. City mouse and country mouse, that sort of thing."

"Courtesy is courtesy. That's what I discovered during my officers' school stint here in France. And not just inside the school, but in all the towns I visited on weekends, and here in Paris. In the French cities there's more formality, but it's the same back in Pointe-à-Pitre."

He maintained a direct gaze, not at all compromising. She huffed demurely. "Well, call it 'formality' if you must, dear Jean. But like I said, she is a sweet, simple girl."

"*Mon Dieu*, Estelle. She's a woman, not a girl. And not a country bumpkin. She graduated university, just like us."

Estelle couldn't bear hearing him talk this way. Good God in heaven! The girl was beneath her in social standing and education.

"Not quite! You have been to officer school and I have attended the Sorbonne," Estelle blurted, then immediately regrated it.

"Give it up, Estelle. Let's talk about something more cheerful, shall we? How do you like your new position with the diplomatic corps?"

Estelle's gut churned. Her man had been so easy going, so suggestable. Now he appeared repelled by her most reasonable statements. She wondered for the first time if she should have remained longer on Guadeloupe, or at least returned there after her imprisonment in Switzerland.

She could have made peace with her parents, locked Jean up tight, maybe even gotten married in a lavish wedding paid for by her wealthy father. Then gone to Paris, to Aunt Sabrina.

To hell with that.

Water under the bridge.

If he knew what was good for him he'd listen. She was the brains, she had the killer instinct in life, in business. She had to get this conversation on track.

She said, "To answer your question, I love my new position – the work and the people. They are all so urbane."

He gave her a look.

She pushed a random thought – revenge sex – out of her mind and said with feeling, "Paris is such a wonderful city. I have my aunt here, and she is a dear, plus my friends at work and around town. I'm quite busy and enjoying every minute."

"So, you aren't thinking about returning home?"

"This is my home now. I thought you realized that. You could move here, you know. Your invitation to the meeting upstairs is a door opening, a new beginning for making contacts in various parts of the government, which could branch out to business."

He looked at her but she couldn't guess what he was thinking.

"I could help you," she said.

"Thanks, Estelle. I'm content with Guadeloupe."

"I'm sure you are, and I am also sure that you would do famously in Paris, even if you determine that you want to continue your career in the Maritime Gendarmerie. You have met people this morning, is that not correct?"

"Yes, of course. French and Mexican, all topnotch."

"And I imagine you will pay a courtesy call to your headquarters and meet important people there as well. These are the movers and shakers, Jean, those who get things done. They are all on their way up, the *crème de la crème.*"

"You paint a compelling picture, but I think you know my answer. I like to feel the sea, the responsibility, even the danger. You don't get that in a desk job."

"Desk job – my goodness. There are plenty of positions in the diplomatic corps alone that involve travel, including at sea and to dangerous places. You might not even have a desk, at least one you regularly use, because you'd be on the road so much."

"I prefer to come home each night, not to sleep in some hotel, living out of a suitcase, in another country. Look, Estelle, I'm okay where I am right now. In the future, I might look for other work on Guadeloupe. It's not that I don't like the sparkle of Paris, but I love the tranquility and friendships of Guadeloupe."

She raised her hand in a signal for peace. "Well, for now let's agree to disagree. I think you would flourish here, and perhaps one day you will investigate the possibilities, but not now. I understand."

His forehead was furrowed. Bad sign. She recalled past arguments during their serious relationship. Jean had been easy-going on the outside, and mostly on the inside as well.

But he had his so-called principles, especially where loyalty was concerned, which had gotten in the way even back then. She had always been able to bring any other man around to her needs, and still could, but not apparently him, if she was up against one of those damnable principles.

A vision of him in bed came to her. She'd always told herself she was in charge, but knew that was not true when they made love. He maintained control, teasing her to higher and higher pleasure, denying her that final release, and finally pushing her over the edge to an uncontrolled peak, physical, mental, and emotional, leaving her drained.

Estelle caught her breath, then realized she had drifted off her agenda. Her stomach was full of butterflies and the rest of her body had responded to thoughts of those wonderful times with this maddening man.

"Jean, why don't we have a nice chat in a more private place, a café? We can catch up."

He gave her a steely look. "I think not, Estelle. We had our good times. But now you've built a life here and I have my life back home."

"With your girl."

"Angela is all woman. And, yes, we are close."

Couldn't he see he was making the mistake of a lifetime? She couldn't help herself. To remain silent was to admit defeat, especially regarding the coming days.

"You'd choose that trash heap of an island over the rest of the world?" she seethed. "Paris could be just the beginning. You could ascend to who-knows-what heights!"

"Stop!" he said.

But she couldn't. "Your career aside, who is this Angela? A sailor that loves turtles, that's who. She has no opportunities, no mountains to climb, nothing to strive for. I have all of those. I'm going places, and you could as well. Let's just talk."

"No, Estelle. And no to a little hop in the hay – which is your usual hidden agenda. That and the pillow talk that follows."

"Then it's *au revoir*?" She couldn't believe it. Was she losing him?

"I think it's more *adieu.* I wish you the best, but we won't be seeing each other again."

She pondered only a second, nodded curtly, and stuck out her hand.

They shook, and turned away from each other, Jean into the crowd, no doubt to search for his little strumpet, and Estelle to locate Maurice.

To hell with you, Jean Aguillard! You are now on my shit list, because in my eyes that is what you are, a piece of merde. *You have not seen the last of me.*

Her expression brightened when she spotted Maurice as he reached the ground floor. She approached him and discretely cheek kissed him, her lips brushing his neck. He bestowed on her an ascetic nod and led the way toward the edge of the crowd. She followed, always the loyal protégé.

He stopped, glanced around, and apparently satisfied that the nearby group of chatting women did not pose a security risk, said quietly, "The meeting was a game-changer, a guaranteed move for me to a position of more responsibility."

She'd heard this before and figured it was a tactic to keep her firmly attached to his coattails. She pointedly looked toward the women and said, "I want to hear all about it. Let's find a little café, alright?"

He shook his head. "No, the subject matter is much too sensitive for café talk."

CHAPTER 14

As he searched for Angela, Jean mulled over the outcome of the Operation Kingfish meeting. He didn't know whether to be energized as a team member or overwhelmed by the impossible scope of his task. The tightness in his chest indicated 'overwhelmed.'

The reason was clear – his single patrol boat was assigned as guardian of the vast area of sea surrounding the islands of Guadeloupe. To transit even from north to south on one side would take too long to catch a speeding intruder. As far as a vessel approaching from the opposite side, even radar surveillance was impossible. He would be blind to all but a limited zone.

He figured he would focus on the main island, with its international airport, the obvious choice for Cabral's supposed route from Mexico to a European destination. Jean would patrol off the west coast of Basse-Terre, covering the direct route from Mexico and the western islands of the Caribbean. In addition, he might request surveillance assistance from near-by islands' coast guards.

Which brought to mind the fact that Cabral used the Dockers gang in Pointe-à-Pitre to transfer his drugs from seagoing to airborne transport. He had to agree with the meeting leader that Cabral's business relationship already offered a secure link for Cabral.

Perhaps, as the Mexican police colonel at the meeting boasted, Cabral would fail to escape their net in Mexico. Jean's conversations with the two Mexican police officers after the meeting indicated their organizations had the man trapped in his villa. They bragged that when the balloon went up, their superior numbers, equipment, and training would overwhelm Cabral's thugs.

"We will scoop him up and drop him in prison," the senior officer had said.

But everyone else Jean had spoken with cautioned that Cabral's wealth, connections, and cunning could reasonably enable the man to engineer and carry out his escape from Mexico to safe haven.

Jean decided he'd hash out the options with his first officer, Georges. Likely, they'd end up going with Jean's initial plan of focusing on the western approaches, but perhaps with an addition or two to improve their odds. Still, his gut told him it was a fool's errand. There were just too many holes through which Cabral might slip.

He spotted Angela emerging from a hallway in back of the reception area. She glanced his way and they made eye contact. She looked worried. They met in the middle of the crowd and hugged, to the amusement of several of the French couples.

"Let's get out of this mob," Jean suggested, and he took her hand, which was clammy. "What's wrong? Are you okay?"

"I'm pissed."

"Oh?"

"It's that woman, Estelle. She's a witch."

"Yes, but with a 'b'." They both smirked and he added, "I spoke with her briefly, and she said you were in the ladies' room."

"Right. She bumped a waiter's tray of Champagne, and it spilled on my blouse. I had to dab it with water and stand under the blow drier."

"She bumped the tray on purpose?"

"Oh yes, and glasses fell and broke on the floor. The waiter gave her a nasty look. I think he knew I was her target. I'm sure the spilled Champagne was a ruse to get me out of the way so she could talk with you alone."

Jean squeezed her hand. "I'm sorry, Angela. She won't do it again."

"Damned straight. I'll whack her with a belaying pin if she gets within five feet of me."

She gave him a lopsided grin, and he laughed.

Angela asked, "So, what did she have to say to you?"

"We only talked for a couple of minutes. The short version is that she wanted me to move to Paris, get a job in the diplomatic corps, and rise to a position of prestige and power."

"*Mon Dieu*! She doesn't know you at all. You'd hate that."

"Right. I told her I was happy on Guadeloupe, and being skipper of LA VIOLETTE – and with you as my lady."

She squeezed his hand. "Thanks, Jean."

"You're welcome. And I meant it all. Especially about you. I told her *adieu* – our paths have parted for good."

"I think you did the right thing, Jean. But how do you feel about it?"

"I feel great – relieved of a task I should have taken care of long ago. Today she came on strong and showed me her true colors, face to face. She made it easy. She's out of my life for good."

"Hmm, we'll see. Maybe not for good."

"What do you mean?"

"She struck me as the type to hold a grudge. And if she involves Guadeloupe in her schemes, she may have an opportunity to get revenge for you dumping her."

"Revenge. Yes, that would be like her."

Angela nodded, paused, and said, "Let's change the subject. You'll be proud of me – I discovered a few things about what your meeting was all about."

"You kept your ears open, asked a few questions?"

"Sort of. I overheard four things: – 'capture,' 'police cordon,' 'Operation Kingfish,' and 'Mexican drug lord.'

Jean gawked.

Angela snickered. "I think the meeting was about a police plan, named Operation Kingfish, and its goal is to capture a Mexican drug lord. Oh, and I also learned his name – Bernardo Cabral."

Jean grinned. "You're right about everything. My gosh. Everyone thought they were being so secretive."

"A word here, a word there."

"I guess. Well, we've got to assume that within hours Cabral will know all about the meeting and the tactics we discussed."

He drew a deep breath and said pensively, "You know, when Estelle and I were going together, we were both young – not so much in years, but in the ways of the word. I was idealistic, and I think she was, well, naïve."

"But you both changed."

"Yes, though looking back, I can tell that back then she was driven and even ruthless when she set herself a goal. Also, she gravitated toward the darker side of life, like dating Vincent Ballou. He was just another punk with a gang tattoo back then, but obviously he was driven as well, and now he's the leader of the Dockers."

"I know," she said quietly.

"Really?"

"He, er, keeps his boat at the marina."

"Wow. Well, stay on his good side."

"I will, believe me. He's a scary guy. But you were saying about Estelle?"

"My point is, she's after power and prestige, and she's succeeding, it seems." He gestured. "See, there she is talking with Maurice Blanchette, one of the French delegates. He seems like a mover and shaker."

Jean gazed at the two, noticing their intense expressions. "He's no doubt a manipulator, just like Estelle." He shook his head. "I'm glad to be rid of her."

"She misjudged you – pushed you too far. You're usually so tactful, you know, always looking for a win-win compromise."

"Yeah, but for that to work, both parties need to give a little."

"Which you've done in other spheres of your life, where your approach can succeed, like being captain of LA VIOLETTE. The crew would follow you into a hurricane if you gave the order."

"Thanks." He rubbed his chin. "Unfortunately, that might happen. A different kind of hurricane. Operation Kingfish is serious business – Cabral is a powerful and brutal man, and the Mexican and French governments are determined and brutal in their own ways. I foresee a terrible confrontation. No compromise."

She gave him an encouraging hug. "You will succeed, Jean."

He smiled, then checked his watch. "Oh, we should leave. I have to visit the Maritime Gendarmerie headquarters and meet the colonel."

"Okay, I can find my way back to our hotel."

They followed other attendees out the door and onto the street, turned right, and walked toward a busy intersection. Jean thought of the coming meeting, which would be awkward enough because he had never met the senior staff and the colonel. But it would likely be even more delicate because he was banned from sharing any information about Operation Kingfish.

A hundred meters from the intersection, Jean pointed. “There’s the Metro in case you don’t want to walk – or you could take a crazy taxi.”

“Maybe I’ll walk a little.” She gave him a peck on the cheek. “See you soon. I’m looking forward to being done with business, and it’s just you and me in Paris.”

He held her hands and gazed at her face. “You know, let’s have a romantic dinner tonight.”

Angela smiled and kissed him. “That’s a deal. And let’s not talk about Estelle or business.”

“Yes – just Paris. And us.”

He hailed his taxi for the short ride to headquarters. Looking back at her, he waved, hoping she didn’t notice the concern in his eyes over the coming operation.

CHAPTER 15

Angela smiled and waved back to Jean, but she was worried about him. The vision of his somber face remained as his taxi sped on its way. *Damn.* The meeting must have revealed that Operation Kingfish was more perilous than he let on.

She wondered about the evil of men like Bernardo Cabral and Vincent Ballou. Vincent she had experienced up close, and had felt his intense and antagonistic aura. But he had another side, the one that had caused him to say he was in her debt for saving his life. As if he lived by a code, however rough and violent.

Did Cabral live by such a code? Did it make any difference? Repaying a debt seemed a poor counterweight to the evil spawned by such men.

Angela was gratified to have Jean as her man. He had his own code, based on integrity and loyalty. Feeling a pleasant tug in her chest, she recalled that Jean, even bearing his new burden, had invited her to a romantic dinner. She missed him being by her side, and wished she could give him a big hug.

She pondered what to do while waiting for him. There were many choices of course. Maybe she should visit an art museum. Jean could only tolerate these in small doses. Or perhaps window shop in Triangle d'Or fashion boutiques, off the Champs-Élysées. Or just sip coffee at a café and watch the world go by – no, that last one needed Jean along so they could chat.

As Angela deliberated, she unconsciously fell in step with other guests from the reception, all ambling toward the busy intersection.

She decided without enthusiasm that she would visit an art museum.

She turned and scanned the crowd behind her, hoping to spot the woman scientist from the reception and invite her to come along. But she only saw strangers and recognized a few details – a hat, a scarf, a mannerism.

Except for one couple, their eyes slanted down. The woman had linked her arm with the man's and they were speaking, their heads close, as if the subject were for their ears only. The woman she recognized as Estelle. The man she could not immediately place.

Were they discussing Operation Kingfish? Maybe.

A voice in her head exclaimed, 'Probably. Most likely. Surely.'

She shushed the voice with an impatient gesture, then reconsidered, deciding it could be a sixth sense alerting her. The voice admonished, 'Go ahead, listen to what they say.'

What the heck, she figured. It would take no time, and even a stray word could be valuable in learning more about the operation, perhaps even Estelle's scheme. And regarding the scheme, was the man involved? They sure seemed like a team, glued together, in their own universe.

Who was he?

Angela rummaged her brain, sensing she had encountered him recently, likely at the reception. She dared to take another look at him, his lips tight, Estelle whispering in his ear. He was tall, thin, an ascetic face, and wire-rim glasses.

Suddenly she realized he was a member of the group of self-important delegates she had spied on at the meeting. Also, he and Estelle had been talking together after the meeting. That's where Jean told her the man's name. Now here he was again and the two looked thick as thieves.

She remembered – his name was Maurice.

Just as Angela again faced toward the busy intersection, she heard him say urgently, "Not here. We must first..." The rest was obscured by footfalls, chatter, and passing traffic. Knowing Estelle, she'd raised the subject of the meeting, impatient to be cut in on details. From his response, Angela felt confident that Maurice was willing to share, at least to an extent. Which made sense, since Estelle supposedly worked for the diplomatic corps.

Angela set her jaw. She would follow them to their quiet place and eavesdrop. She felt a chill, part excitement and part dread.

What if Estelle should see me? Worse, what if she made a scene?

Even now, Angela was worried Estelle would spot her through a gap in the crowd and recognize her. The woman was a fashionista and likely remembered what everyone wore. Particularly the blouse on which she'd spilled Champagne. Angela reached into her bag and pulled out a light-weight beige raincoat. She slipped it on, then removed her scarf and stuffed it into the bag. There was nothing she could do about her hair, combed and straight.

Angela continued to match her pace with the others, forcing herself to remain calm, to maintain a relaxed posture.

The intersection was very near. Soon, the crowd would disperse. Some to the Metro, some to taxis and others continuing on foot, strolling in the mild weather. Angela's eavesdropping plan appeared doomed.

Her gut ached.

At the edge of the intersection, the traffic light turned red and a large truck stopped, belching diesel fumes. There were a few exclamations and chuckles at the stench. Most of the crowd increased their pace, seeking clean air. One couple aimed for the crosswalk in front of the truck.

A distraction.

Angela quickly followed the couple, and a moment later they were passing the front of the truck, looming above them. Pedestrians approached from the opposite side of the street, and a few people from the reception trailed behind Angela.

She turned sharply left as soon as she passed the hood of the truck, and made her way to the back of the vehicle. She took care to remain close, so its square bulk hid her as Estelle and Maurice continued to walk down the sidewalk.

When she emerged at the rear of the truck, she held her breath against the foul exhaust odor and scanned the sidewalk. The crowd from the reception had nearly passed and she joined up at the end, still not seeing anyone she knew. She searched for Estelle and Maurice up ahead, spotting him first, his height giving him away, then Estelle.

The couple reached the intersection and Angela's heart thudded as she waited for them to make their decision – left, right, or straight ahead. They chose a wide, tree-lined boulevard to the right, bordered by stately nineteenth-century apartments. She paused to let her quarry gain distance from her. Their shoulders were not touching, and Estelle no longer had his arm, which indicated they were saving serious conversation for their destination.

There were no stores or restaurants on the first level of the apartment blocks, just imposing wooden doorways every half block and gracious stone-framed and white-curtained windows in between.

No nooks for her to duck into.

Even the tree trunks were too thin to offer cover. There were no crowds to blend into, only one other person, walking her dog. Angela gritted her teeth and followed Estelle and Maurice, fifty meters back, feeling very exposed but hoping the distance would be enough to keep them from noticing her.

She considered crossing the street, but decided that could draw attention because then they only had to turn halfway around to spot her.

After an interminable five minutes, they crossed the boulevard onto a side street, heading toward the Seine. Beyond them, on the other side of their side street, stood a large building that Angela recognized as the Trocadero, some sort of palace, she thought.

Angela crossed the boulevard, following them onto the side street that she now saw was leading past a wooded park located behind the massive Trocadero.

She quickened her stride, and when she entered the park, declared by a sign as 'Jardins du Trocadero,' she caught a glimpse of the couple, walking along a path. Only a few other people were present, each in their own world. The setting seemed perfect for the privacy Maurice appeared to be seeking.

The artful arrangement of trees and bushes and flowers, and the view of the timeless Eiffel Tower invited her to enjoy this calm island within the busy city. But as she anticipated the coming exchange of forbidden information, her heart rate increased.

She was sweating as well, and worried that her risky gambit could end up being a waste of time, and worse yet, a cause of embarrassment.

She hung back, only close enough to her quarry to verify their location. After another minute, they turned left onto a path bisecting the park. Angela scampered to the turn-off as they departed from the path and entered a shaded glen, trees and shrubbery surrounding a grassy center.

She carefully followed, and saw them sit on a bench facing the grassy center of the glen. They settled in and Estelle placed her hand on his thigh. He patted her hand affectionately and she smiled.

Angela smirked.

She retraced her steps to the path directly behind the Trocadero. After waiting for a woman to pass, she edged into the foliage, skirting bushes and mature tree trunks, working her way closer to where she judged they were sitting.

Moving slowly, she soon heard their voices and corrected her navigation several meters to the left. She stopped and knelt behind a large bush emitting a tart scent. A bird called and a wisp of breeze brushed her sweaty cheek.

She gazed through the tangle of limbs and leaves. Maurice had scooted closer to Estelle on their bench. He put his arm around her shoulders. Estelle turned and murmured something to him. They became silent, apparently settling down from the events of the meeting and getting their thoughts together.

Maurice looked and acted the part of a nerd genius, the center of his own universe, with Estelle no more than an orbiting moon. *Hmm.* Obviously, the elegant Estelle had set aside the need of a partner with social graces, because her goal was undoubtedly to further her career, and this man must fit the bill. Probably a high-level manager.

Judging from the couple's body language, Maurice seemed to value Estelle's judgment, and Angela was sure that Estelle more than upheld her half of the partnership, with cunning and intelligence.

At length, Maurice said, his voice muted amid the rustle of leaves, "I want to brief you on details on the meeting."

"Good. Then I'll tell you about my plan for our way ahead, you know, with Charles and his people." She continued, her voice sweet,

"I'm glad you were our representative at the meeting. You have a photographic memory and, may I say, a devious mind."

"Ha! Devious. I love that." He paused for a second, then added, with a transparent lack of sincerity, "I wish you could have been there."

"I guess they described the particulars of how we will coordinate efforts with the Mexican diplomats?"

"Right, with the help of the usual viewgraph presentation."

"Was there a timeline?"

"Yes. The Guardia Nacional will move on the villa within a week."

"The Guardia Nacional – is that their version of our Police Nationale?"

"Yes, I believe so. They've laid on the men and equipment to do the job, that's for sure. I talked with the Guardia Nacional colonel after the meeting and he bragged about having a mobile command center, two armored cars, and snipers on the roofs of the houses facing the villa, all primed for the assault."

"Assault! Not knock on his door with an arrest warrant?"

"Good grief, no!"

"Why? Does he have his own army?"

"You don't understand. Cabral is a drug lord. He is surrounded at all times by a gang of heavily-armed bodyguards, especially now, holed up inside his villa. These guys are paid to defend him at all costs. Cabral must know they won't win against the police, but they will at least delay the invasion long enough for him to escape."

"But he's surrounded. How could he escape?"

Maurice shrugged. "Maybe with his own armored vehicle, crashing through the police lines, then quickly switching to another vehicle, then a plane, or boat, or even hide in place. The man has choices, and money is no issue."

"How does France come into this?"

"My thought is that the Mexicans are bringing us on board mainly as a political favor, so we can claim partial credit for his demise."

Estelle said, "Their other motivation must be that Cabral's drug smuggling route goes through Guadeloupe – a part of France."

"You're right. So bringing us onto their team obligates us to be ready to intercept him on French soil." He looked her in the eye.

"You're from Guadeloupe. What do you think the police will do down there? Have you heard from anyone?"

"No, I'm disconnected from that place. I grew up there, but it's been a long time. I'm not in touch with anyone."

Maurice snapped, "Disconnected! That's a laugh. With your history with that gang, with the drug scene, with Jean Aguillard – you must have made contact with someone." His tone darkened into anger, "You are absolutely connected and you have something up your sleeve to make yourself look good. And does not include me."

"No, Maurice, that's not – "

He gestured dismissively. "You're lying, my dear Estelle. I can hear it in your voice. Don't you know that I am an expert at picking out the liars in my presence?"

"Back off, Maurice. Of course I know people from Guadeloupe, and I do communicate from time to time. I simply did not want to bog you down in irrelevant details. I even know Vincent Ballou, the leader of the Dockers gang. They smuggle drugs from Mexico to Guadeloupe.

"I also know Jean Aguillard, the captain of the island's only armed patrol boat. I haven't talked with Vincent for years, and we parted on very bad terms. Jean and I were an item, but our long-distance relationship is now finished. I hope never to see either of them again."

"So you say."

She stood, posture rigid, and hissed, "You need to recognize the truth when you hear it."

She stalked out of the park.

Maurice remained.

Angela thought she heard him mutter "Bitch!"

CHAPTER 16

As Estelle walked the few blocks toward the Trocadero Metro station, she contemplated her departure from Maurice. She had left him with his mouth slack and anger in his eyes. Did he believe her? Feigning innocent anger had been the best defense she could come up with but now it felt weak.

God, what a fool I was.

In the meeting, Maurice had been briefed on Jean, and likely Vincent as well. The man had set a trap and Estelle walked straight in. He won, catching her in a lie, badly damaging her credibility. She tried to shrug it off, reminding herself that she would soon be rid of the man. But Maurice's snare, coming out of the blue, had unbalanced her. Sure, she was going to dump him, but meanwhile he could have been of use in her scheme.

Damn him, his ego and his flaccid attempts at making love! All he craved was power. The bastard would now be seeking to replace her, robbing her of the initiative.

Screw him.

I need to focus.

She forced herself to recognize her progress to date. Long hours on the Internet, confidential conversations with her contacts, examining interoffice memos and position documents. Digging up personal information on Cabral, even to the number of his personal mobile phone.

She'd also researched the successes and failures of the Mexican Guardia Nacional in capturing high-profile criminals. Finally, she studied strengths and weaknesses in the cooperation between the French and Mexican governments. All this she had carried out with an eye toward designing the best escape plan for Cabral, from villa to safety abroad.

She arrived at the Trocadero Metro station, paused at the entrance, and pulled out her mobile phone.

Because one gaping hole remained in her plan. She pressed speed-dial to Aunt Sabrina.

"Hello, my dear Estelle."

"Hi, Aunt Sabrina. Can we talk?"

"Yes. Perhaps at our favorite café?"

"Okay. I'm at the Trocadero. See you in twenty minutes?"

"Good. See you then."

Estelle returned her mobile phone to her purse, frowning. Her aunt had grown more cautious, suggesting a meeting instead of talking on the phone. Which meant she suspected her line had been tapped. 'One of the prices we pay,' the woman would put it, in a tone of decorum. Estelle would add curse words.

She made the journey to the Metro station closest to their favorite café and walked the final distance. She chose a table away from other patrons, gaining privacy. Their usual waiter appeared and she gestured that she would wait to order.

Aunt Sabrina arrived five minutes later, bestowed cheek kisses, and sat with a flourish, eyes bright and attentive.

She said quietly, "So, the awaited meeting has taken place and afterwards Maurice has told all."

"Yes." Angela updated her aunt, then said, "There is more to add, I'm afraid."

"Hmm, I thought I heard concern in your voice during our phone conversation. Perhaps having to do with Jean?"

"My gosh, Jean! How could I have forgotten to tell you? At the reception, I managed to get rid of his little plus-one, then Jean and I had a private discussion."

The waiter arrived.

Sabrina smiled, "I'll have coffee, please."

Estelle said, "I need something stronger. A glass of sauvignon blanc for me."

"Oh well, me too."

The waiter nodded and departed.

Sabrina asked, "You were saying?"

"Jean is so uptight."

"My dear, he is military. All he sees is black and white, and not the wonderful panoply of shades of gray on which we thrive."

"Poetically put, Aunt Sabrina. In the end, he pooh-poohed even the thought of moving to Paris and joining the diplomatic corps. He would not consider leaving that scroungy island."

"And his plus-one? She has stolen his heart?"

"Yes, they are two do-gooders with no imagination. She's a turtle-saver. God. Let the freaking turtles fend for themselves."

"Very practical."

"Jean is a lost cause. He dumped me."

"Yes, he has chosen the island girl. But we knew that was coming. What was she like?"

"Pretty, but not entrancing like us. She's intelligent, I'll give her that, though she possesses only about the same level of cunning as Jean. And damn him. I offered him a wonderful career on a platter. I have the contacts and I could make things happen."

Sabrina waved a dismissive hand. "Jean is history, my dear."

Estelle felt a tightening in her chest. "He's history all right, regarding any help I have to offer him."

"Including your hand in marriage."

"Yes. But he's burned all his bridges. I'll have the last say."

Sabrina's eyes widened. "Revenge? But, dear me, that takes time and effort."

"I know. Is he worth it? Is that what you're asking?"

"Perhaps. It would complete the circle for that relationship. But worthwhile only if you can fit your revenge into your more important plans as a simply-orchestrated side note. Otherwise, you must drop the idea. You already have so much on your plate."

"You're right, as always. Well, there is something else I wanted to tell you – I broke up with Maurice."

"My goodness. What happened?"

"It was at the Trocadero, in that little park. We sat on a bench and he described what happened at the meeting. Then he asked if I had contacts in Guadeloupe. I guess he figured I could talk with them and relay useful information to him about Cabral if he did travel to the island.

"I said it was all history, I had no contacts. But the little snake reminded me that I certainly knew Jean, who was at the meeting, and Vincent. I made a scene and left him sitting on the park bench."

"Not ideal."

Estelle shrugged. "It's his loss. Anyway, I'll blame him for the breakup, even though he was right about me lying. After my plans succeed, I'll switch my allegiance to Charles and forget all about Maurice."

"But he will have an axe to grind."

"Let's forget those two men," Estelle said dismissively. She drew a breath to clear her mind. "I want to ask you about air transport."

"Ah, I did have an opportunity to talk with my Algerian friend."

"The one who doesn't like the French?"

"Exactly, and who can blame him, after the French bungled Algeria? He is a businessman with contacts all over Europe, and owns several private jets. One is equipped to fly to America, where he has other contacts. He was delighted to help, and even said he would pay for pilot and crew, and fuel."

"My gosh! What a godsend. You've filled the final gap in my plan, as you promised. I need that fast transport, and the range. Thank you so much, Aunt Sabrina!"

Their wine arrived and they toasted.

Sabrina put her glass down. "You are more than welcome, dear Estelle. But you do understand, don't you, that you will be in debt to my Algerian friend? And are you comfortable not knowing his name? Though I'm sure you realize that is frightfully sensitive information, keeping in mind that he wants to be distanced from any official enquiries regarding this scheme of yours."

"I know I'll be in his debt, and that's okay. When I'm with Charles, I'll be able to help him, I'm sure."

"And the name?"

"I don't need to know his name. He may remain a man of mystery. *Hmm*, does this arrangement mean he and I will communicate through you when he needs that favor?"

"Yes. It will be better that way, with me as your intermediary."

Estelle nodded, though a tremor in her hand told her she had stretched her trust of Sabrina to its limit. Her beloved aunt would have the power to ruin her. Estelle concluded that she must keep her eyes open for an opportunity to gather dirt on Sabrina. Two could play that game.

Aunt Sabrina was talking.

"Just contact my Algerian friend's pilot to arrange details." She passed Estelle a neatly folded piece of paper. "Tell him when you need the plane and where you'll be visiting. Oh, and confirm where the plane should collect you. I suggest the general aviation airport my friend usually uses – Toussus Le Noble, forty kilometers outside the city."

Estelle tucked the paper inside her purse and finished her wine. "Aunt Sabrina, you have been most generous. Now I owe you even more."

"You are welcome, Estelle. One day I shall call you and ask a special favor."

Estelle suppressed a shiver, for her mentor's eyes held a cunning glint.

CHAPTER 17

Bernardo Cabral, head of Mexico's most powerful drug cartel, was a success by any measure – market share, government connections, and cash flow. Especially cash flow. The money poured in – dollars and euros and a half dozen other currencies. He lived in royal luxury and was planning his next super-yacht, to be built in Europe.

But in the past tumultuous days, all that success had vaporized into a mirage, worth a tinker's damn.

I am nothing more than a prisoner in my own house.

He gazed through the full-length bullet-proof windows of his paneled study, looked down at his manicured garden, its grass, hedges, rare orchids, and stately trees.

The view normally calmed him, reminding him of treks through mountain rainforests. But today it mocked, for the rainforests would remain and he would go.

Yes, I must go – but not to prison. This is my vow.

Cabral thought back on his efforts to ensure his freedom from the current foray by the Guardia Nacional. He had endured a half dozen unproductive interviews with fixers, each promising a secure escape to a non-extradition civilized country. But each with a flawed plan.

He turned from the window to the other person in his study, Enrique Santos, his lawyer, a partner in one of the most prestigious legal firms in Mexico. Once an athlete, he was now nearing retirement and had gone to fat. But he possessed a steel-trap mind and was willing to do Cabral's bidding, no matter what law he had to circumvent, as long as he could distance himself and his firm from prosecution.

The man sat on a couch, nursing a single-malt scotch. Cabral sat opposite him on the twin of that couch, its burnished white leather squeaking as he settled in.

"Enrique, what is the situation out there?"

"Well, *Señor*, until last night, it was only the sentries and their marked cars from the Guadia Nacional, but during the dark hours they have installed snipers to cover every meter of your villa wall, and parked not a block away several vehicles which portend ominous events in the coming days."

"What vehicles?"

"Two armored cars, a command vehicle, and several Jeeps with mounted machine guns, plus a bus that appears to be outfitted as a living quarters for a squad of police. This according to their colonel, who I know."

"So, they are tightening the noose."

"*Sí*, but they will not move until the government completes certain legal formalities, on which they are taking exceptional care to do correctly within the letter of the law. My contacts will inform me when this is complete."

"So, what is their next step?"

"They will request an arrest warrant. They need that in hand. I will be informed immediately, and at that stage will contact you."

"When?"

"Within two days, maybe less. After you receive my phone call, you can expect them to execute the warrant within minutes. I believe they will send a police car with escorts, using sirens and speeding, to hand-deliver the official paper copy of the document to the police outside your villa."

Cabral gestured in disgust. "*Dios mío*. What are my options?"

"For you to remain in Mexico, you have run out of options. You must get to a non-extradition country if you are to stay out of prison."

"How about negotiations? Didn't we decide that was viable?"

"I am sorry. We are beyond that. All our potential allies have been neutralized, taken out of the lines of action, removed from authority. All except Miguel, and he – "

Again, Cabral gestured in disgust. “Miguel has disappeared, I know. Kidnapped, murdered, arrested, whatever. But he’s gone.”

Cabral observed that Santos’ left hand quivered, a sign of his extreme nervousness. *He is remembering how I deal with failure.*

After a moment, Cabral said, “Alright. Keep me informed.”

“*Sí, Señor* Cabral.” Another hand quiver. “I will do so, but I must inform you that my own position is becoming tenuous.”

“What? I pay you and your legion of lawyers a fortune.”

“Yes, and now we are visited too often by officials. One day about possible tax evasion irregularities. The next day due to lost documentation on your big construction project in the city. And on it goes.”

“Great, just great. So we’re both under pressure. But I’m facing a hell of a lot worse consequences than you. Deal with it.”

Cabral pointed a finger at the man, angry at him, angry at the police, angry that his damned finger was shaking. “On second thought, get the hell out of my house. I will make my own solution.”

Santos’ voice had a pleading tone. “I can still help, as we discussed. Using my contacts to keep you informed. I told you about the meeting in Paris. It took place several hours ago.”

“No, you don’t help. You only deliver bad news. Leave! You are fired.”

Santos edged toward the door, his face a sickly gray. A guard on the other side must have spotted him on the security camera because door opened, revealing three heavily-armed men in black tactical gear.

The lawyer managed a quick, “Very well. I will send you my final invoice.”

Cabral yelled, “Don’t bother. I refuse to pay!”

Santos scuttled out of the room. The door shut silently.

Leaving Cabral alone.

He shook his head, grasped the scotch decanter and hurled it against the paneled wall. Glass exploded across the polished floor, staining the wood and carpet.

His mobile phone sounded the ring-tone of his government spy in Paris. The line was secure – supposedly.

“*Sí*, this is Cabral.”

“I have news of the meeting with the French. Nothing new except one thing.”

"Tell me good news."

"This could be good news. It is a possible lever of influence on the island of Guadeloupe."

"Where we transfer drugs."

"Correct. At the meeting a new man was present. He wore civilian clothes but he's an officer in the French Maritime Gendarmerie. Captain of the armed ocean-going patrol boat LA VIOLETTE."

"What was the context? Drugs or me escaping by boat to Guadeloupe?"

"The second, but it was clear the French know about the smuggling of drugs to their country through Guadeloupe. That is why they are in the operation."

"Can this guy be bought?"

"I have done preliminary checking, and according to a contact I have on the island, the officer is completely dedicated to the service."

"Does he have a family, a wife?"

"Parents yes, but no brothers or sisters. He does have a girlfriend."

"Okay, if I need to I'll have the gang guy, what's his name?"

"Vincent."

"Yeah, I'll have him kidnap her. That'll turn the captain around. Keep me informed."

"*Sí, Señor* Cabral."

CHAPTER 18

When Jean left the Maritime Gendarmerie headquarters, he texted Angela. 'Just got out. Let's meet in our room.' Suddenly impatient to see her, he bypassed a Metro station and hailed a taxi.

He entered their hotel room bearing a bouquet of six red roses in a glass vase, picked up from a vendor in the arcade.

"Oh, they're beautiful! Thank you, Jean. Are we free now?"

She had showered and looked luscious, wrapped a hotel bathrobe. He smiled, and imagined her without the robe.

"Yes. Paris is ours to enjoy."

She hugged him tight, her hair smelling fresh. They kissed and kissed again. Only with great reluctance did he stand back, hands gentle on her shoulders to admire her.

He wanted her.

Badly.

"I made dinner reservations," he said, noticing his voice was a little high-pitched.

"At a restaurant?"

"Kind of. It's a Seine River cruise with dinner. We have reservations for six o'clock."

"On one of those long boats we've seen on the River?"

"Yes."

She nodded innocently, but her red cheeks revealed what was on her mind. He embraced her, felt her slim body, imagining her with nothing on. In bed. The fluffy robe rumpled on the floor.

He murmured hopefully, "I think we have time."

She leaned back but still close and gave him a lecherous look.

He gazed into her hungry eyes and brushed a hand along her cheek. Adjusted a strand of her hair. Saw her chest rise as she caught her breath.

She said in a hoarse voice, "Yes, definitely enough time."

Jean had to hurry to shower and dress, and he laughed with Angela at the late hour. He called down to the front desk and asked the clerk to hail a taxi, which they jumped into, and were on their way.

"Can you be at Port Solferino in seven minutes?" Jean asked the driver.

"Ah, oui, *monsieur*. Even six minutes is easy for me!"

And the man was off, his eyes darting left and right, then at the traffic ahead.

Jean leaned back in his seat and put a hand on Angela's knee. "We need to talk seriously for five minutes. Did you remember anything else about the operation, other than what you told me in the embassy?"

"No, but I did learn a couple of things after you left to visit headquarters."

"Okay."

"Remember that thin man you pointed out when you came down from your meeting? He was talking with Estelle."

"Yes, Maurice. He's a member of the French delegation."

"Well, I spotted Maurice and Estelle walking together among the crowd leaving the Mexican Embassy. They were a bit behind me, with people between us. I put on my raincoat so Estelle couldn't recognize me by my dress. Then I dodged around a big truck at the intersection where you got on your taxi, and I followed them."

He suddenly looked concerned. "You're serious? You followed them?"

"I'm sure they didn't see me, especially since all their attention was on each other, walking close and whispering. I stayed well back as they continued on foot to the Trocadero, where they sat in a little park. I hid in some bushes and spied on their conversation."

"Good grief!"

"Yeah, cloak and dagger."

"But you were careful?"

"Yup, there's no way they would have seen me. They were so engrossed in their own conversation, I don't think they once looked over their shoulders. Though they did stop talking when someone walked by."

Jean shook his head. "You are amazing."

"Thanks. Anyway, I heard enough to convince myself that Estelle really is up to something. But probably connected to the operation in some way rather than directly involved with it. It's hard to say exactly how. Whatever it is, she's not sharing it with Maurice. At first, she didn't even admit to knowing you."

"Did Maurice catch her on that?"

She nodded. "Yes, he seemed to be biding his time, waiting in ambush. He called her a liar. When Estelle realized her mistake, she put on a show of being upset and stormed away, leaving him."

Jean shook his head. "Between the reception and the Trocadero you learned a tremendous amount of information – it's almost like you'd been at the meeting yourself."

She blushed at the compliment, and Jean wondered what else she'd done to gain all that information. He wouldn't put it past her to have disguised herself as a waiter. But he didn't want to know – he was just happy she hadn't been caught.

He said, "So, one minute Maurice and Estelle were thick as thieves and the next, she lied to him and could well have destroyed their relationship. That couldn't be good. I think you're right about Estelle being up to something. And it's got to include Guadeloupe. Why else would she try to cover up that she knew me?"

Angela nodded. "What do you think we should do?"

"For starters, we need to be careful. Cabral has his finger in lots of pies, and he plays for keeps."

"Can you ask around?"

"Let me think about it. I met other people at the meeting. Though frankly, I doubt if they can add anything to what we already know. Let's keep our ears to the ground when we return to Guadeloupe. Talk with our friends. Though not your customer at the marina, Vincent, because he could be part of Estelle's scheme, and he's dangerous."

Jean felt the taxi slowing and noticed the driver was pulling up to a pier at which several dinner boats were moored.

The man turned in his seat. "We have arrived. Six minutes, *oui*?"

Jean nodded with a grin. He paid and tipped the driver. Angela exited and Jean admired her *derrière*. His mood switched from official business to romance.

Or maybe it was lust.

Whatever.

She smirked at him, having read his mind, and took his hand as they trotted to the gangway.

Jean gestured to the sun, still high. "I wanted us to have an after-dark cruise and admire the city's romantic lighting, especially the Eiffel Tower. But sundown is not till almost ten o'clock."

"That's fine. I couldn't last that long for dinner."

As they stepped onto the pier, Jean surveyed their boat, a sleek version of the river barges that hauled cargo along the Seine. Her superstructure was glass, like a greenhouse, with an enclosed bridge poking up, all sufficiently low to pass beneath the bridges of Paris.

At the short gangway, he checked in with an officer, who welcomed them aboard. Jean figured they were probably late, because the man immediately gestured to sailors forward and aft, who released mooring lines.

A horn blared from the bridge.

Their table for two was forward, with a panoramic view. Most of the other tables were for six guests, and Jean mentally thanked the secretary back at headquarters who had made their reservations. God bless the Parisians and their love of romance.

Engines rumbled, and the boat curved away from the pier to the center of the Seine, cruising upstream at a stately pace. A waiter arrived with their order for a bottle of Sancerre. He displayed the label, uncorked, and tipped a little into Jean's glass for taste and approval. Jean nodded; the waiter filled both glasses and departed.

Jean grinned at Angela. "The French wine ritual."

She laughed. "A lovely custom."

Jean raised his glass. "To us."

She touched her glass to his and they sipped, smiled, and caught their breath from mussed sheets, speed-dressing, and running to the taxi.

The waiter re-appeared. Angela decided on beef for her main course and Jean chose duck.

Jean admired Angela, beautiful in the early evening light.

She touched his hand across the table. "Jean, thank you so much for inviting me to come with you to Paris, and for this romantic dinner. I love you."

"I love you, Angela, and you're welcome. I love seeing you happy."

They toasted again and their appetizer arrived, an exquisitely presented arrangement of seasonal vegetables with a flavored oil topping.

But Jean's attention remained on Angela.

"I'm glad you decided to stay on Guadeloupe for a while and not continue to sail to other islands."

"Thanks. Me, too." She cocked her head to the side, as if in deep thought. "Hmm, was it the weather that kept me there? No, it's the same as the rest of the Caribbean islands. How about Catherine, my good friend? Nope. The food?" She gave him a teasing look. "Maybe the food."

He shook his head in mock dismay.

She raised her finger as if in discovery. "Ah, yes, I remember now. A dashing Maritime Gendarmerie officer!"

She squeezed his hand.

He wondered if she could see his cheeks, which felt overheated. They gazed at each other for a minute amid the soft tinkle of silverware and murmured conversations of the other guests.

The waiter arrived with the main course. Almost reluctantly, they glanced at their plates, then each other, and snickered.

"Thank you for that 'dashing' part, Angela."

"Mmm, you're welcome. I guess we should eat this delicious-looking meal."

They began, and agreed the food was as tasty as it looked. When they finished, the waiter removed their plates and set a cheese course.

Jean said, "You know, the meeting and the visit to headquarters have gotten me thinking."

"About your career?"

"Yeah. Captain of LA VIOLETTE is as high as I can get until someone above me retires."

"I think you would be a great commodore."

He nodded his thanks. "Well, I might reach commodore, or I could push for an assignment at one of the other bases in France or on another island." He paused, looking at Angela; inviting her thoughts.

"I think you'd be good at either one of those options, or at something else." She rubbed her chin. "But not working in the diplomatic corps. You are way too practical, and the blowhards would drive you crazy."

"You're right. There's plenty of time to figure this out, but I wanted to share my thoughts with you."

She gave him a look and he wondered if he'd made the wrong assumption, thinking they were more than friends and lovers.

Her lips quirked. "Jean, you look so serious."

"I guess."

"Thank you for sharing. I have the same kinds of thoughts. I like working to save the turtles, and I like sailing, but I wonder if there is something else waiting for me, like starting a professional career."

"Sure," he said. "With your university degree you could pursue so many careers – marine-related, or even business. You're great with people, and practical. Look at how you're managing the marina." He smirked. "All while you're listening patiently to the owner, who doesn't know anything about the care of boats. And you picked up right away on the campaign to help the turtles."

They nibbled on the cheese course and finished their wine, then the chocolate tart and praline dessert arrived.

"Wow – death by chocolate!"

"Yum," she said, and shot him a warning look. "Better guard yours, bud. This looks sooo good."

"Let's order Cognac, to celebrate our visit to Paris."

The waiter smiled in approval and returned a minute later, setting the distinctive balloon snifters down with a flourish.

Angela sipped and made a face. "Wow, that's strong."

"It is, but it goes down well, don't you think?"

She sipped again and half-closed her lids. Then she leaned forward and spoke quietly, replacing his question with one of more importance.

"Do you feel that vibration in the deck, coming up all the way through the chairs?"

"Sure. It's the diesel engines. They're kinda rough."

"I wouldn't call it quite that."

Her voice was low and urgent, her eyes burned into his.

He thought, *Mon Dieu.* Talk about lust.

"The vibration, Jean."

"Yes?"

"It's turning me on."

CHAPTER 19

Angela awakened, disoriented by screeching birds, then remembered she was no longer in her quiet Paris hotel but home in her bungalow on Guadeloupe. She reached across her bed, feeling only a tangle of sheets.

Oh yeah.

They'd arrived at her place in the wee hours because of an Air France flight delay and went right to sleep in each other's arms. Which was very nice.

Not so nice was Jean's phone buzzing at four in the morning, calling him to respond to a distress call.

Merde. After a magic night with Jean, they were back to real-world problems. The worst being terrible dangers from Operation Kingfish and Estelle and Cabral, maybe Vincent as well, and who knew what other people or gangs.

She felt an odd claustrophobia, as if she were captured inside an evil bubble. Reminding her of visiting remote beaches with her friends to protect the turtles, when they were suddenly attacked by Delian and his gang.

Angela quickly showered, and over coffee she planned. Her goal was to dig up new information about Cabral and the others, especially about Cabral's escape route and whether that route included Guadeloupe. She was after anything of value – whispers, rumors, facts.

Deciding to start her quest by visiting her good friend, Catherine, Angela punched speed-dial on her mobile phone and gulped the last of her coffee.

"Hi, Angela. Back from Paris?"

"Yes. I loved it. Jean and I actually had special time alone. It's quite a romantic city."

"Hmm, I'll bet. I'm busy this morning, but I want to hear all about it."

Angela's throat went dry. "Catherine?"

"Uh oh. Problems?"

Angela shuddered. "Yes. Big time."

"We need to talk?"

"Could we? It involves a situation. Nasty people on our island."

"I'll cancel my class. No worries. Shall we meet somewhere in the city?"

"It'd have to be in a park or another open space – no people to overhear what we're talking about."

"How about my place? I'll run out for croissants. Bart is on a painting job, so it'll only be us."

Angela let out a breath. "I love you, Catherine."

"Ha, I love you, too. See you soon."

Catherine's flat was its usual friendly self, and Angela had to smile at its floor-to-ceiling mural of beach, palm trees and a setting sun. It was a creative work by Bart, and fill-in coloring by Catherine and Angela.

After cheek-kisses, Catherine laughed. "Do you still like our work of art?"

"Yes, and Bart was a dear to let us help him out."

"The man doesn't have a stingy bone in his body. He shares everything."

"Except – "

Catherine smirked. "Right! He doesn't share me with anyone."

"That's what I love about our guys. They love us so much and we love them."

"True blue. Though they do spend too much time working."

"Well, that's part of our job, to entice them to take a break and enjoy us."

"Bravo." Catherine led the way to the kitchen table, where two mugs of coffee were steaming, accompanied by plates holding almond croissants. She said over her shoulder, "I heard you bounding up the stairs, so I poured our coffee."

They sat, sipped, and nibbled.

Catherine asked, "So, what disaster are we trying to prevent from happening on dear Guadeloupe?"

Angela looked her friend in the eye. "You must promise not to tell a soul."

"I promise. God, you sound so serious."

"Sorry."

Catherine made an erasing motion. "It's okay. And don't worry – I can keep a secret. But you made me a shiver. Your eyes sort of sparkled, and I swear I saw little motes of gold."

Which told Angela she felt the danger so deeply it sparked her animal-instinct emotions. She tried to calm her nerves with sip of coffee, but the cup shook so badly she placed it back on the table.

Catherine frowned and patted Angela's hand. "Take a breath. There's no hurry. Just the two of us."

Angela breathed slowly.

Her hand quit shaking.

But a creepy feeling enveloped her and lay heavy, like a soggy fisherman's net. She drew another breath, closed her eyes, decided she had no choice but to let the net stay, and move ahead. She had things to do.

"It's about a Mexican drug lord, a man named Bernardo Cabral."

Catherine's eyes widened.

"Yeah, *that* Bernardo Cabral. Jean's business in Paris was to attend a secret meeting between the French and the Mexicans, to figure out how to capture him."

"You're scaring me, Angela. This sounds like war. Cabral must have his own army and he'll fight."

"He could fight, but the Mexicans think he realizes he'd lose in the end. They're going to try to capture him at his villa, but if he escapes the villa, they're sure he'll try to escape to another country. The scary part for us is that he might well follow his drug smuggling route, which is through Guadeloupe."

"Is Jean supposed to capture Cabral at sea before he gets here?"

"Yes, you guessed it. But if he fails, Cabral and his thugs might end up here."

Catherine's forehead wrinkled. "But, *Mon Dieu*, we don't need that kind of excitement." She touched Angela's hand. "Now I know why you're so serious."

"Yeah. When two countries work together like this, it's a big deal. By the way, they gave it a name – Operation Kingfish."

"It sounds way out of our league."

Angela waited a beat, then said, "But there's a way we can help."

"How?"

"By learning all we can from people on the island who might be involved in Cabral's escape. As we gather bits and pieces of information we can let Jean know. I suggest we start with Estelle."

"Estelle? She's long gone. Besides, she's just a, well, a rich pain in the ass. Wait a minute – didn't you tell me she works for the French diplomatic corps?"

"Yes, and she's part of Operation Kingfish, which means she knows everything the French and Mexicans are planning. Her boss, a guy named Maurice, is one of the key diplomats on the French side."

"Okay." Catherine gazed thoughtfully into her coffee.

"Also, I found out that she's planning her own scheme, maybe connected to Operation Kingfish. She's keeping it secret from Maurice."

"Blackmail, to get even richer?"

Angela shook her head. "I don't think she's after money. She thrives on power."

"Well, you're right about the 'power' part. She was so bossy in school."

"Okay, you went to school with her, but I just met her a couple of days ago. Oh, the good news is that I saw her for what she is, and so did Jean. She tried to nab him but he told her *adieu*."

"Farewell? Like forever?"

"Yes. He saw through her manipulative ways and this time it was crystal clear that the only person she loves is herself."

"Good riddance."

"Yes, as far as her having her claws in him. But she's still dangerous, and up to something, like I said. Tell me about her, how she thinks. Maybe we can guess her plans."

"Okay." Catherine sipped her coffee before starting. "I knew her since we were in grade school. We were in different circles, because her parents were rich and powerful and I was just a local kid. She ran with other rich kids and ruled a clique of three other girls.

"She also had evil friends from the wrong part of the city. Street hoods who got expelled from school. The worst of them was Vincent. Anyway, she seemed to crave living on the edge."

"No safety rails?" Angela guessed.

"Exactly. She was a risk taker. If the reward was big, then count her in. Though on the surface, she acted like a cherished, polished, educated daughter."

"And she glommed on to Jean, right?"

"Yes."

"But how about Vincent?"

"Ha! She was a chameleon, with multiple personalities, each one a perfect fit to the group she was running with. She kept each group separate from the others. So Jean and Vincent never saw each other."

"There was no competition between Vincent and Jean for her attention?"

"None. Their paths never crossed. It was like one was a turtle and the other a seagull."

"Wow."

Catherine nodded. "We knew about her gang personality from street gossip, but experienced her 'school' personality first-hand. She made a project out of charming Jean and convincing him she loved him. My little group joked about it, because it seemed so obvious, yet Jean didn't seem to have a clue.

"She'd wait for him after class, and outside of school she invited him to family events, like lawn parties. You could see he was in a daze, like the frog kissed by a princess. They became serious, and everyone figured they'd get married."

Catherine was silent for a while, then said, "You know that girl, Emilie, from your turtle-saving group? Well, her brother, Delian, was in the same gang as Vincent."

"The Dockers?"

"Right. Emilie told me stories she'd heard from her brother about Estelle. He said she was like a partner with Vincent, and even more daring and sneaky than him when the gang was causing trouble."

"But at the same time she was officially with Jean in a serious relationship?" It seemed inconceivable to Angela.

"Right. Jean seemed convinced she loved him and that he loved her. My group was sure the relationship with Jean was a plot by Estelle to trap a good-looking man who was socially adept, and too trusting to realize he was being manipulated.

"Married to him, she'd have a cover to move in society. I don't know whether she wanted to go to Paris, though we did hear she had a wild-woman aunt there.

"She was never caught doing gang stuff until she finally broke a law and her family shipped her off to a school in Switzerland." Catherine laughed. "She could easily fit into being a spy if it were war time, or into crime if not, such as drug selling, counterfeiting, or smuggling."

Frustrated at hearing Jean cast as a fool, Angela shook her head. "God, Jean's dad was – and still is – a respected *quimboiseur*."

"Yes, I've met him. He's a combination shaman, sorcerer, and healer. He's very respected on the island, as is his wife, who helps him out in his practice."

"Well, I wish they would fight evil people like Estelle."

"Me too," Catherine said with sympathy. "But your mom is an *Obeahwoman*, right? What does she do about evil?"

Angela shook her head in frustration. "You're right. There's only so much they can do. I guess Estelle drew Jean into her web and he felt like he was on cloud nine."

Catherine smiled. "Then she was sent away, and he was no longer in her orbit. You arrived on the scene."

"Yeah, I guess."

"Think of it Angela – good triumphs over evil."

"You're right."

"Yes, I know. And you know some other good news? Jean was a romantic, that's why he fell for Estelle."

Angela grinned. "He still is."

"You see? That's the good news. She didn't turn him into a sour person, she was only a lesson in what's worthwhile."

"So is Bart – a romantic. He's a sweetie."

Catherine smiled. “I know – I love it. But we’re really not talking about Jean and Bart.”

“Right. We’re talking arout the enemy. Anyway, I think we have Estelle figured out.”

“I agree. How about Vincent? He’s now the boss of the Dockers. What do you know about him?”

“Not much. His gang is into drugs, though I don’t know details. I’ll ask Emilie.”

“Or I can. I know her pretty well.”

“Okay, but here’s the thing about Vincent. He is one merciless bastard.”

“Wow. Tell me what you really think.” Angela shuddered. They might be sitting in her friend’s cozy kitchen but she still felt vulnerable to the evil forces they were discussing.

“Okay,” Catherine said, “Here’s an example. About a year ago a street punk vandalized Vincent’s car, which showed serious disrespect, because that car was like a badge of authority in the gang world. It was a twenty-five-year-old Cadillac, fully restored, including an old-fashioned whip radio antenna. The street punk snapped the antenna and left it dangling. To show how tough he was, I guess.”

“So, Vincent found out who it was?”

“Yes, that same night. One of the Dockers heard the guy bragging in a bar and told Vincent. Vincent waited until the punk left the bar, then he grabbed him and hauled him back to his car. A couple of Vincent’s gang members followed along. They reported that Vincent ripped the top part of the antenna free of the wires and used the jagged end to gash the punk’s face from his eye to his jaw.

“The punk screamed and gushed blood, but Vincent refused to stop the bleeding or even call an ambulance. He just wiped the blood off his hands with the punk’s shirt and walked away.”

CHAPTER 20

Estelle rinsed her Pinto Envol hand-painted porcelain coffee cup and placed it on the drying rack in the compact kitchen of her Paris apartment. She stepped into the living room, paused to straighten a David Michel ceramic vase, and frowned at the long shadows cast by the late afternoon sun. Time was running short.

She sat at her dining table, her 'war room.' From one of a dozen neat stacks, she selected an architect's drawing of the interior layout of Cabral's villa in Mexico City. She grimaced at what it had cost her – an hour on the couch of the senior security officer at the Mexican embassy.

But worth every sweaty minute.

The drawing provided insight into how Cabral's villa was protected from attack. The outside walls were made of poured concrete. There were no windows on the ground level and only two external doors. Windows on the second level provided clear, overlapping fields of fire against attackers. Once inside, interior walls of concrete promised a strong defense against hand-held arms. Right-angle turns in hallways enabled a fighting retreat.

Disappointingly, there was no hint of a safe room, escape tunnel, or heavy-weapons cache. She was sure some or all of those features existed, and concluded that various dimensions of rooms and halls must have been fudged on her drawing to disguise their presence. She figured other defensive features existed as well, such as remotely-activated anti-personnel explosives, trap doors over pits, and perhaps even poison gas.

She rubbed her chin, studying the drawing, memorizing the layout. Absent were flowing fountains, marble statues, grand staircases, or a ballroom. No bowing to art, music, and gracious manners. Cabral, she was certain, aimed only at creating an image of dominance, not of sophistication.

Estelle replaced the drawing, reached for a fresh burner-phone, and keyed in a number she had memorized. There was a single low-pitched beep and she pictured Cabral reaching for his secure and private mobile phone.

He wouldn't recognize the number but, she calculated, would be curious enough to wonder who it was.

He answered, his tone uncertain, that of a man under duress. *"¿Sí? ¿Quiene es?"*

Knowing he spoke excellent English, she said, "Good morning, Mr. Cabral. I am calling about Operation Kingfish." Her voice sounded confident and her delivery urbane.

"What do you have to say to me about Operation Kingfish?" He sounded angry, but remained on the line.

"I have a way to take you to safety."

"Who are you?"

"My name is Estelle Boucher. I am a consultant to the French diplomatic corps. A warrant for your arrest will soon be issued, followd immediately by a visit from the Guardia Nacional. I know a way you can escape to a safe, non-extradition country. Shall we meet face-to-face? I believe you will like what you hear."

He said, all bluster, "Okay, I will meet you. Here in Mexico City in my villa. Tomorrow."

"Very well. I will arrive in Mexico City tomorrow morning at nine o'clock. I will call an hour prior to landing at Toluca International Airport. I assume you will have someone meet me."

"Yes. My chief of security. He has blue eyes, a scar on his left cheek, and speaks passable English with a German accent."

"He's German?"

"Yes. Very efficient. The car is an armored Mercedes. You will be completely safe."

"Alright. Until then."

She set the phone on her desk for later disposal, tented her hands, and reviewed her impressions from the call. The powerful and feared Bernardo Cabral had immediately accepted her offer to listen to her proposal. Which confirmed he had already explored all his options to remain in Mexico, including legal maneuvers, bribery, and threats. He had also no doubt listened to, and judged flawed, several proposed escape options and found himself at the end of a blind alley.

Right where she wanted him.

Cabral would check on her position within the French diplomatic community and note her reputation for success in complex situations. Then Estelle would arrive at his villa holding all the cards. He would huff and puff and she would act as if he were in charge. Just like with Maurice.

She reflected on her choice of Toluca International Airport, the most popular executive and general aviation airport in Mexico City. Importantly, it was among the busiest in the country. Chances were good that Cabral kept a personal plane there for local travel, likely now under observation by the police.

Using another burner phone, Estelle called the mysterious Algerian's pilot. She'd already briefed him of her international flight needs, and now wanted to confirm that all was in order for the trans-Atlantic flight to Toluca.

"This is John," he said when he heard her voice.

Her lips quirked at the thought of him feeling the need for a fake name.

"Hi, John, it's Estelle. Can we meet at our agreed-upon location in an hour?"

"*Oui*, I have confirmed my flight plan to our destination at – "

"No, not on the phone."

"Yes, I understand. Alright. One hour."

As she waited for her taxi, she remembered the Algerian's warning, as retold by Aunt Sabrina: "You will find your pilot waiting for you at the airport. He is medium height with a trim build. No gut, and no mustache. If you do not see such a person, quietly walk away and don't look back. The police will be watching."

Estelle arrived at Toussus Le Noble Airport a few minutes before three o'clock, paid off the taxi, and entered the modest terminal building.

Uninvited, an irritating vision of Jean popped into her head. He and his little girlfriend, walking hand in hand, eating at a charming café. Sleeping together.

Merde!

Jean was too damned handsome and dashing to waste himself on that girl. But he had turned hard, and not the good kind – the self-thinking kind. Their parting still rankled her. She should have had the last word. Should have dumped *him*. In spite of Aunt Sabrina's advice, Estelle nurtured the idea of sweet revenge. She'd take him down a peg or two while she was in Guadeloupe with Cabral.

Estelle passed through the terminal building, which included the control tower, a restaurant, and a café. She found John nursing a coffee at an outside table, apart from others. He raised his hand a few centimeters in recognition and she joined him. They shook hands, she sat, and ordered a coffee.

As Sabrina had relayed to her, he was medium height and wiry. She hadn't mentioned his searching eyes. He looked to be about sixty years old and well used, but she figured some of the wrinkles could have come from years of flying. Oddly, he wasn't smoking a cigarette.

He got right to business, speaking quietly and making eye contact. "The aircraft is fully fueled and ready. She is parked on the apron." He pointed to a wide asphalt surface between terminal and runway on which three planes were tied down against being tipped over by wind. A fourth plane, not tied down, stood by itself.

"That jet, blue on the top, white on the bottom?" she asked.

"Yes. She's a Palatus PC-24, Swiss-made. Very dependable, and great for landing on unimproved runways, which I think you requested?"

She nodded. "And it can carry plenty of fuel?"

"It can. This one is fitted with an eleven-hundred liter, extra fuel tank. We'll need it, and it's a good thing you and your luggage are our only loads. Don't worry, we're within margins, and the forecast headwinds are not too high. Though there is weather passing through Guadeloupe – a tropical storm with squalls."

"So, how many hours will it take to get to Mexico City?"

"I figure eighteen hours, including brief layovers at the Canary Islands and Guadeloupe for fuel."

"And if we take off in the next few minutes, when will we arrive?"

"Immediate take-off with give us twenty-four hours available for making a touchdown in Mexico City at nine in the morning local time."

"So you and I will be in the airplane for twenty-four hours straight"

"Unless you want to pause. Sleep at a hotel. That would mean extending the arrival time. Of course, you can depart the plane and stretch your legs when we stop for fuel."

"Alright. No hotel. But when will you sleep?"

"I'm okay. I was in the military. I'm accustomed to staying awake and alert for long periods."

"You flew in the military?"

"Yes, for the French Air Force. Fighter pilot." Those eyes drilled into her, as if to add, 'I don't want to talk about it.'

She shrugged inwardly. *Okay, a man of few words. As long as he gets me where I need to be.*

He nodded toward her luggage, a single carry-on. "Is that all you're taking?"

"Yes." Her coffee arrived and she took a sip, decided she did not have the time to spare, and stood. "Let's go. There's food and drink on the plane, right?"

"Yes. The galley is fully stocked. And there's a lie-flat couch with pillow and blanket if you want to catch some sleep. Though no flight attendant." He looked at her with his head cocked to one side. "That's what you wanted, right?"

She gripped her carry-on, glanced at their plane. "Yes. Perfect."

The air over summertime France was bumpy, then bumpy again in and out of the Canary Islands. Guadeloupe was blustery on landing and hot and humid when she briefly deplaned to stretch her legs. Take-off was bumpy, through the remnants of a tropical storm.

During the two multi-hour legs of the flight, she tried reviewing her notes but was too keyed up to focus.

Sleep was out of the question.

Estelle was fully awake as they completed their final leg, flying above the Caribbean, with the coast of Mexico a vague silhouette on the horizon. She drew a breath and exhaled. Gazed out the window at the blue sea.

Exactly an hour prior to touchdown at Toluca International Airport, Estelle removed another fresh burner from her designer black leather satchel and punched in Bernardo Cabral's private number.

CHAPTER 21

Jean gripped the cool steel bulwark of LA VIOLETTE's flying bridge, scanning the ocean ahead and to either side. Basse-Terre's gray bulk lay ten kilometers to starboard. Black clouds scudded overhead and long rollers marched westward, causing the vessel to roll on her northerly course. He wiped spray from his face, pleased to see the last of the tropical storm.

He put binoculars to his eyes, blinked away the fatigue from most of the night on watch, and focused on the western horizon. All gray, with no sign of the two contacts being tracked on radar.

Still too far for a visual.

As he awaited the next radar report, he thought longingly of Angela and their enchanted time in Paris. He felt close to her, and missed having her by his side to share a sight or simply hold hands. He prayed for an uneventful day, followed by joining her at her bungalow, if only to share the same bed for the night. Then back to sea, lately lashed by squalls and the resultant sailors in distress.

The intercom buzzed. "Captain, this is bridge. Two contacts, range eighteen kilometers, bearing two seven five true. They are separating, one continuing east with apparent destination Deshaies, the other apparent destination south of Basse-Terre, perhaps Les Saintes."

Jean keyed the mike. "Very well. Continue to track both contacts." To his helmsman, he ordered, "Make your course two seven five, speed fifteen knots."

"Aye-aye, sir, turning, two seven five, speed fifteen knots."

The vessel swung to port, now taking seas from astern and pitching into the swells, raising white water over the bow and dousing his foul weather gear. A cold trickle of seawater traced down his chest. He tightened the towel around his neck, knowing it would soon be too wet to block the spray at this heading.

Footsteps sounded on the steel deck to his left. Georges approached and saluted. Jean returned the salute.

"You look concerned, *mon capitaine*."

Jean shook his head. "It's been a long night, hasn't it?"

Georges brushed his bristly chin. "Yes, but at least we saved some people, *n'est-ce pas?*"

Jean nodded absently, then resumed scanning the rolling sea. They had found a tossing sailboat in the pre-dawn darkness, her rigging in shambles. He'd sent his engineman over on the RIB, and minutes later the sailboat's engine cranked over. Topside damage kept her from sailing, but the engine would carry her to safe port on one of Guadeloupe's islands.

Jean said, "You're right. Georges. It feels good to rescue people."

"*Oui*, much better than fighting smugglers." He looked at Jean's binoculars. "And now, we are again on a rescue mission?"

"No, I wanted to take a look at the western approaches to Guadeloupe, try to figure out how we could best ambush Cabral if he escapes from Mexico and tries to route through Guadeloupe."

"Any thoughts so far?"

Jean shook his head. "None, except that we don't have the coverage. We need more boats. Helos would be nice as well. I've made calls to local islands and they said to let them know when we receive an alert."

"But?"

Jean shrugged. "They're always busy. Maybe they'll give us a few hours of help here or there, but probably not even that."

"This Cabral, he is very important?"

"To us he is. I guess not so much to them."

"How close are the present two contacts, *mon capitaine*?"

"Last report, eighteen kilometers."

"So, our horizon is ten kilometers, no?"

Jean glanced at the sea, "Yes, up here on the flying bridge. But depending on their height, I'm hoping to spot their top hamper in a couple more minutes. We're on a collision course of about thirty knots."

Georges said, "This picture of the three vessels, the speed and headings, it is all in your head like a picture, *n'est-ce pas vrai?*"

"Yup. Minus the air clogged with spume."

"Ah, the realities of life."

Georges raised his binoculars.

The minutes ticked by. *So much damned waiting in this business.*

The speaker sounded, "Captain, this is bridge. Two contacts continuing on course as before. The northern contact is now on collision course with us, range nine kilometers."

"Very well." To Georges, Jean said, "Do you see him? Probably a yacht or sportfish."

"Perhaps. I believe I see him a few degrees off our port bow."

Jean squinted and panned his binoculars ten and then twenty degrees in an arc, scanning the horizon. "Yes, I've got him."

"A sportfish, pitching, disappearing, then topping a roller, yes?"

"That's him. We'll check him out."

"A smuggler, you think?" Georges asked, still looking through his binoculars.

Jean shook his head. "Probably legit."

When the distance to the boat decreased to two hundred meters, Jean reversed course and matched the other boat's course and speed. Jean and the helmsman descended to the quiet enclosed bridge and hailed the boat on VHF radio.

"This is Lieutenant Jean Aguillard of the French Maritime Gendarmerie. I request you slow your vessel to five knots and order all hands on deck, with your helmsman at the controls on your flying bridge."

Jean ordered LA VIOLETTE to remain fifty meters off the boat's port side. He and Georges swept the boat with binoculars, eyes open for weapons of any kind, especially automatic and heavy caliber guns or RPG launchers.

After a minute, Jean said to Georges, "These guys look like fishermen on vacation. One guy's swigging beer. Pot bellies instead of muscle."

Georges muttered. “They sure don’t look like hostages, you know, with hidden pirates pointing guns at them.”

“No.” Jean spoke on the radio link, “Thank you, captain. Have a smooth trip.” To his helmsman, he ordered, “Wait until he ups his speed and clears us, then steer zero-nine-zero.” To the radar team he ordered, “Stop active tracking of both contacts, set a course to Deshaies.”

Helmsman and bridge affirmed, and a minute later, LA VIOLET pointed toward the seaside town located on the north-west coast of Basse-Terre.

Georges asked, “Are we paying a visit to the Maritime Gendarmerie brigade at Deshiaes?”

“Yes. I want to alert the chief.”

CHAPTER 22

LA VIOLETTE lay moored to the pier at Deshaies, the vessel bumping rhythmically in time to sea rollers entering the harbor area. Jean arranged several pages of scribbled notes on the wardroom table, along with three cups of steaming coffee. He made eye contact with the other two men present – Georges and Chief Petty Officer Lambert. CPO Lambert, crusty and dependable, was the man Jean had come to visit. He commanded the Maritime Gendarmerie Autonomous Territorial Brigade, Deshaies.

"Thanks for meeting with me," Jean said. "I know you have a hundred other things to do."

"No worries, sir. What's up?"

"We have a situation, so secret that they sent me to Paris – "

"France? They invited you to France? Why didn't they invite the commodore?"

"Yes, Paris, France, and I'm also surprised they didn't choose the commodore instead of me. Probably because I'm captain of the only patrol boat on the island. They needed me directly in the know. The operation – classified – is to prevent a drug lord named Bernardo Cabral from getting to Guadeloupe."

"Isn't he the guy behind the smuggling?"

"Yes. The police plan to arrest him in Mexico City, but they realize how slippery billionaires can be. They want a backup plan in case he gets away and decides to route through Guadeloupe."

"Damn."

Jean stared at Lambert. "I'd appreciate your help on the western approaches, Chief."

"But do I understand I will not get orders from the commodore?"

"Nope. I take my orders from Paris – from a diplomat. Not even our HQ are briefed."

"Sounds fishy to me."

"Me, too. The commodore's not happy, being out of the loop, but he's accepted it, given the short timeframe and the importance of Cabral."

Lambert sipped his coffee. Set it on the table and looked at Jean. "This is all about that mysterious subject you mentioned on the radio, right?"

"Yes, it is. We can expect no help from other islands. I've called them and they've got their own problems. If they can spare a boat or helo, they'll help."

"Yeah, I get it. Too much to do, too few resources. Can't blame them. But you realize my boat's only a little twelve-meter job, not a patrol boat."

"She's seaworthy and you and your crew are seasoned. Plus, you have radar, comms, and can help search."

Jean tapped his notes, "Just now, out there off Basse-Terre, we tracked what could have been two boats apparently together, heading toward Guadeloupe. Then they split, one toward Deshaies – "

"Right," Lambert said. "She moored here, in the protected harbor, less than an hour ago. Harbormaster said they were Americans on a bare boat charter. Four guys, who looked innocent enough, out to fish and drink beer in the Caribbean sun."

"Good, that's what we concluded when we checked them at sea. Then the other boat continued south."

Lambert shrugged. "What's your point?"

"I'm thinking that Cabral will come – if he comes at all – with two boats. One will be a decoy, the other will carry him. The one carrying him will look innocent, and the other will look fast, seaworthy, and decked out with the latest radar and comms. They'll come together, from north, west, or south, and split up as they near Guadeloupe, just like those two today."

Lambert shrugged. "A diversion, inviting you to follow the souped-up boat while the other one continues to Grande-Terre, to drop Cabral off for his flight to freedom. Okay, I'm in. If the commodore asks, I'll tell him we're on a routine patrol. What do you need me to do?"

"Nothing fancy. Both our boats will look about the same size on Cabral's radar, thanks to your radar reflector."

Lambert nodded. "But what's the point? So Cabral thinks he has two larger boats after him instead only one. What does that buy us?"

"It buys uncertainty on his side. He'll be desperate and on a tight schedule, on a route full of risks of being caught. Now he sees he's under full observation."

Lambert grinned. "He's primed to make a mistake."

"Right."

"Okay, what's our timeline?"

Jean said, "The Mexican police will storm Cabral's villa in a the next few days. I'll get word of the results – whether they captured him or he got away. If he got away, time will be of the essence. I think he'll fly to an island near us, then take a fast boat here, then a plane to his final destination."

"So we need to get out there on patrol within hours of receiving word he's on the run?"

"Yes. It'll take a plane about five hours to get from Mexico to a near-by island, then another five hours on a fast boat to reach Guadeloupe."

"Why not fly directly to Guadeloupe? Land on one of our islands or, heck, on a straight section of road?"

Jean said, "Because the flight controllers at our main airport on Terre-Grande will be on the lookout for a private plane during that time period."

Lambert smiled. "You've thought a lot about this."

Jean nodded. "Every minute. I figure you take the north and west approaches. I'll take the southern tip of Basse-Terre and the islands south of that.

"How about the east?"

Jean shook his head. "He'll be in too much of a hurry to spend time on that much of a detour."

"Okay, I'll brief my guys to be on call and I'll keep mum on sharing details until we're well to sea. We'll be ready."

Jean rose. "Thanks, chief. I owe you one."

Lambert grinned at Georges, "You heard him. Sounds like some serious bar-hopping to me." He scratched his chin. "I think I'll select a fine scotch at our first stop."

Jean had attempted to cat-nap on their return to base, but was awakened by a call from Commodore Lavigne, ordering him to report to his office immediately upon mooring.

Now he sat in the outer office, the commodores' yeoman focusing on his computer, and voices being raised behind the door to the inner office. Two alpha males.

Jean checked his mobile phone, finding one message from Angela, saying she was 'poking around' and had news for him. He frowned, praying she was not calling on gang members, especially Vincent, with his hair-trigger temper. He keyed his response, 'Sounds good. See you for dinner. Be careful.'

The phone buzzed on the yeoman's desk, and the man picked up, listened, then said to Jean, "The commodore will see you now, sir."

Jean knocked twice, heard "enter," and stepped into the office. The commodore sat at the head of his conference table, his face bright red, lips tight.

The tall, thin diplomat that Jean remembered from Paris, Maurice, sat at the other end of the table. Maurice wore a well-cut suit in tropical-weight fabric. Three others were in the room, two men and one woman, wearing suits as well. Jean figured they were Maurice's staff and was a little surprised not to see Estelle. He wondered if she and Maurice had parted ways after their argument outside the Trocadero.

The commodore gestured toward vacant seat to his left. Jean sat. "I ordered you here," the commodore said to Jean, "because the situation has changed, and – "

"Not changed – matured," insisted Maurice, his head tilted back and looking down his nose, as if addressing a subordinate.

Commodore Lavigne stiffened.

Maurice continued, alternating eye contact between the commodore, the woman staffer, and Jean. "I have been placed in charge of all activities involving French participation in Operation

Kingfish on Guadeloupe. I have briefed Commodore Lavigne on all particulars relevant to him.

"The situation in Mexico City is fluid, and we could be called for support on an hour's notice. I am here to ensure prompt action is taken the moment we receive a call to action."

"You mean, if Cabral escapes from Mexico?" Jean asked.

Maurice gave him an irritated look. "Yes, lieutenant."

The commodore jolted forward and glared at Maurice. "He's 'captain' of a French Maritime Gendarmerie patrol vessel. He will be addressed as such, no matter what his rank."

Maurice smirked, cut his eyes to his staff, of which only the woman looked back. He said, "Very well, 'captain' it is."

The woman joined her associates in examining the top of the table.

Jean thought, *Even his staff are painfully aware that he's a pompous bull in a china shop.*

Maurice continued, his tone condescending. "As I was saying, if Cabral does escape, and we are notified that he might be transiting by sea to Guadeloupe, we must be ready for immediate action. Pursuant to that, we must ensure a direct line of communication from Mexico City to Paris and then to Guadeloupe. The formal communications between the diplomatic side in Paris and the Maritime Gendarmerie takes hours at best. With me here in charge, the transmission of information in both directions will occur in a few minutes."

He paused a beat and stared at the commodore. "With all this in mind, I order you, commodore, to direct everyone under you to report any applicable information directly to me, beginning immediately. I must know what is happening here, with regard to Cabral's drug-smuggling accomplices, who are his most likely partners in escaping through Guadeloupe."

"I will notify my personnel to report to you directly," the commodore said in the frosty tone Jean recognized only too well. "Presently, there is nothing to report, especially in view of having just been informed by you of only the barest of operational details."

Maurice nodded curtly. "Very well. I will use your office as my command center. I, or one of my staff, will be here twenty-four hours a day." He turned to Jean. "I want to be kept updated by you, 'captain,' on all your operations, whether or not they appear to involve Cabral. As well, you will provide notice to me before you get underway on LA VIOLETTE."

Jean answered in his no-nonsense 'command' voice, "Yes, sir, I will keep you informed. We often must leave port for emergencies on a moment's notice. Waiting at the pier is not an option."

Maurice's tone turned icy, "You will call me before departing the pier. I will tell you my decision and you will obey – whether to remain at the pier, wait for my arrival, or depart."

Jean glanced at the commodore then at Maurice. "My official chain of command is not through you, sir. It is through Commodore Lavigne. Also, I remind you, sir, that I am the captain of LA VIOLETTE. I am responsible for life at sea in an emergency, especially in cases where speed is of the essence, which is nearly always the case."

Maurice went rigid.

As did his staff.

The commodore said, "I'm sure we can – "

Maurice shouted, "I am in charge of this operation! Not you commodore, and certainly not you, captain of your tiny patrol boat. You will remain at the pier until I order otherwise."

Jean started to rise, thinking he might return immediately to sea and effectively close this petty argument and avoid risking lives because of the man's ego.

The commodore, probably imagining his career ending in flames, gestured for calm said, "Perhaps, sir, the situation could be clarified if your superiors provided sufficient direction to my superiors in Paris."

Maurice slapped the table.

His assistants flinched, except for the woman, who calmly took a breath. She'd obviously witnessed him in action before.

She looked at Maurice and then the commodore, and said, "I could make the appropriate calls."

Maurice wiped spit from his lips. The commodore's face faded to a shade of pink.

"I have the phone numbers in hand," she assured her boss. "It will only take a little while."

All of which convinced Jean this woman had indeed taken Estelle's place as Maurice's trusted advisor. And she was likely clutching his coattails, cunning and merciless, just like Estelle. Jean also concluded that Maurice was here for one purpose – to boost his career by claiming credit if Cabral were captured on Guadeloupe.

He reminded himself to tread carefully around the three of them, and also to keep his ear to the ground regarding anything Estelle might be up to on Guadeloupe. If she had been banished by Maurice, she would be looking for another, more powerful, mentor.

He was glad Angela was asking questions.

CHAPTER 23

Aggravated by the damned police and politicians, and bleary-eyed from another sleepless night, Cabral sat across from Estelle Boucher on the twin couches of his study. She was pulling papers from her satchel and laying them on the coffee table between the couches. She looked obnoxiously calm and collected, unlike his lawyer and unlike every other recent visitor.

She had called his private mobile phone an hour prior to landing as promised, and had landed at nine o'clock sharp. Her palms when they shook hands were dry as dust.

He rubbed his cheeks absently, realizing he had forgotten to shave. *Dios mío.*

His manservant arrived with coffee and pastries and set them on the table between the couches. Cabral looked at Estelle and raised his eyebrows. She responded with a smile, indicating that she would be fine with coffee. The manservant departed.

Damn. On time. Dry hands. Well-dressed.

It all made him feel uncomfortable. Out of the driver's seat.

Perhaps she was all sales and no delivery. On the chance that she was as competent and cool-headed as she made herself out to be, he decided to start soft.

"Did you have a good flight?"

She replied in her calm voice, "I must say that I like flying in the smooth air at altitude, above the summer heat drafts of France and the Canary Islands, and the scraps of the latest summer storm over Guadeloupe."

"You came by private plane of course?"

"Yes. With extended range, excellent speed, and able to land on unimproved runways."

"Which will be part of my escape plan?"

She cocked her head slightly. "Perhaps. Depending on several things we will talk about, with final arrangements depending on your approval."

He said, "I must inform you that I have made several calls since our conversation yesterday. To, er, learn more of your credentials."

"Good. I was hoping you would, to put our relationship on a firm professional footing."

He was impressed, and also chagrinned. He was used to being the smartest person in the room. The best prepared.

She asked, "Having considered what you heard from your phone conversations about my credentials, what is your conclusion?"

"Depending on my agreement to your plan, and to your fee, I will hire you as my, shall we say, guide."

"My fee is one million euros, half in my account today, and the other half when you arrive at your country of residence."

He considered briefly. A million euros was a pittance. She could have insisted on ten times that amount. But it was a reasonable number – professional, and not greedy.

The half and half part, that was the risk. He shrugged inwardly. Sure, he was at risk regarding the first half – that she would leave him high and dry, or even hand him over to the police. She was at risk for the second half – that he would be on safe ground and refuse to pay.

He admitted admiration for her business acumen in his world, where to break a promise was to invite revenge, and to keep a promise invited future cooperation.

He extended his hand. "Very well."

They shook, and again, her palm was dry.

She handed him a slip of paper. "Here are the particulars of my account." She waited for him to tuck the paper into a pocket, then said, "I suggest we begin by concurring on your destination outside of Mexico. I believe an excellent choice would be Switzerland. English is widely spoken, the culture is European, and – "

He gestured impatiently. "Switzerland is fine with me. Have you thought through the necessary arrangements?"

"Yes. As far as getting there, I have located a place with an airstrip from which a person can cross undetected into the country from France. You would be provided with a local guide and take a walking trail. There will be no passport check."

He nodded. "That sounds good. I'm also concerned with the long term, after I am in the country."

"Long-term prospects are excellent. The Swiss are protective of their national prerogatives, and in particular the idea of extradition, which is what we're talking about, right?"

"Exactly."

"It turns out that the Swiss do not have extradition treaties, though they do have their Mutual Assistance in Criminal Matters law, which could be used to arrange for extradition."

"I think that is very bad news. What other countries are there, where I would be safe from the Mexican authorities?"

She shook her head. "Not to worry. There are options in Switzerland. For example, it is very difficult to extradite a Swiss citizen."

"So you'll find someone to forge a Swiss passport for me?"

"Good Lord, no. You would need much more proof of citizenship than a forged passport. But there are better ways to guarantee your ability to legally remain in the country. You will begin by hiring good lawyers, and I have several firms in mind. Also, you will lay groundwork, such as demonstrating the ability to support yourself, by depositing money in Swiss banks."

He smiled tentatively, "Which I would do anyway. Please continue."

"You must file papers to establish residency and then begin the process of obtaining citizenship. You must not conduct any illegal business in the country. There must be no traceable link to your present enterprises. Can you arrange that?"

He made a dismissive gesture. "Yes, of course. That is easy."

"Good. You also must nurture relationships within the appropriate Swiss governmental bureaucracies, so that you will receive special consideration should any legal questions arise.

"In general, you must keep a low profile. The Swiss are a modest people and appreciate their potential new citizens being modest as well. Also, hire locals – lawyers, bankers, even staff members for your villa. Finally, contribute to political campaigns."

"Really, politics? Is that not high profile?"

"No, you keep it between yourself and the person receiving the donation. It is part of relationship building."

"Alright. That sounds well thought out." He glanced at his watch, brow furrowing. "We can discuss details later. What else?"

"I have several questions, then I'll describe my plan."

He rose, poured a scotch, offered her one, which she refused, and he sipped and sat.

She asked, "Do you have an escape tunnel? I have studied your residence drawings, but I did not see a tunnel."

Cabral took another sip, swallowed, and said, "Of course there is a tunnel. It is a necessary precaution. The tunnel leads to a modest home in an adjacent neighborhood. The home is occupied by a husband and wife on my staff." He shrugged. "For obvious reasons, the tunnel is not shown on any documents."

"Good. We will make use of the tunnel. Another question: is there someone you trust completely who can serve as your double? Not at close range, but say if he were driving a car and observed by a surveillance camera."

He cocked his head. "That's easy. My gardener. He is the same height and build as me."

"Good. Please tell him that you will need his services, and arrange for him to wear the same color and style clothing as yours when you depart."

He nodded.

"A final question," she said. "My sources indicate that your point of contact on Guadeloupe for, er, transferring product, is the leader of the Dockers gang – Vincent Ballou. Is that correct?"

Cabral's lips tightened before answering. "Yes. He is the person in charge, and the person I trust should I ever be on the island. How do you know of this man?"

"I know him from when I lived there. Please contact him and authorize me to be your representative."

"Alright."

"I must talk with him face-to-face regarding details of your transit through Guadeloupe. My meeting will only take an hour, at the small airport at Saint-François."

Cabral nodded.

"Now," she continued, "I will present my plan. Ask questions, because you must understand it well, and agree."

He listened, asked several questions, and argued a point, but in the end gulped the remainder of his scotch and nodded. "Yes, I agree to this plan of yours."

She gathered her notes and stood.

His eyes widened. "Are you quite sure a face-to-face meeting with Vincent is necessary? A phone conversation surely must be sufficient."

"Sorry, but the devil is in the details, as the saying goes. I might need to personally check on certain things, such as the boat he'll use to take you to Guadeloupe, perhaps the car he'll have waiting on Guadeloupe, and making sure his driver is properly briefed."

"*Dios mío*, this is so complicated! I have just been thinking – why not simply fly from Mexico to Guadeloupe, refuel there, and continue to France?"

She faced him and spoke slowly, with care. "During those first few minutes and hours after the police lose you, they will scour the land, ports, and airports with a fine-toothed comb. Any flight heading out of Mexico toward the east is at risk of being intercepted. Heading in another direction and circling back to Guadeloupe would put the plane beyond its fuel range. And that reminds me. Another purpose of a face-to-face meeting is to agree on back-up arrangements."

"Backup? It sounds like you are inviting failure of your plan."

"No, it's real life. Things will go wrong and you need other options each step of the way. Remember, our adversaries are smart and motivated, and when things start happening, they've got a vote in the action."

He put his hands up in mock surrender. "Okay, okay, I agree. I know all about that."

"But there's good news. As a consultant to the French diplomatic corps, I developed key elements of the plan to capture you if you escaped from Mexico. That plan has weaknesses we will take advantage of. I have thought about this longer than they have."

"You are saying that you have faith in the plan we just discussed?"

"Of course. It's a good plan and it might need adjustments to counter actions of the police. That is not a problem. Let's remember we are more agile than they are. They must communicate with superiors before making changes to their procedures, then brief their assets in the field, all of which gains us time. We make and execute our changes immediately."

"And again, you insist on the necessity of this meeting with Vincente?"

"Vicente and I need to look each other in the eye. He and I are taking great risks, and we must be in complete agreement in order to act quickly when events occur."

He rose and stood at the window, ignoring the exotic greenery, but rather drawn to the tall security wall. The only barrier between himself and the feared Guardia Nacional, gathered outside like killer dogs, awaiting the command to strike.

He had a vision of being bundled into a military plane, clothed in a prisoner's jumpsuit with a black bag tied over his head, handcuffs chafing his wrists. The airplane's engines racing, the plane accelerating down a bumpy runway, then slanting upward and reaching only a modest altitude. Droning onward for an hour.

Strong hands grasping his arms, a fuselage door opening, the inrush of roiled air. A frog-march through buffeting wind, and a shove. Into nothing. Tumbling, hands bound, legs flailing, shrieking out his final minute on earth.

He turned and faced Estelle, who stood, her expression expectant, satchel in hand.

He said with great reluctance, "I understand. I await your return."

She smiled reassuringly. "Thank you. I will leave immediately. Oh, there is one more thing."

She told him in three sentences and ignored his protests as his eyes darted around the room, pausing on a painting, a small statue, and his empty glass.

CHAPTER 24

Angela spent the morning at the marina, inspecting boats and moorings, and greeting owners. Throughout those hours, her mind was casting about for ideas of how to ferret out Estelle's plans concerning Guadeloupe. Angela was certain the woman would show up – her conversation with Maurice at the Trocadero screamed loud and clear that Estelle demanded control, including being present when things went south.

At noon, Angela called Emilie, her friend from turtle-saving days, and asked if she could visit for a confidential conversation. Emilie said okay, and Angela hopped on her TaoTao street scooter and sped to Pointe-à-Pitre.

On the way, she recalled Emilie's torn loyalties, between their group battling to save the sea turtles, and her brother Delian's turtle snatchers, who murdered the creatures for shells and meat. Emilie had agreed to spy for Delian, and used the money to feed herself and parents.

She now had an honest job, and Delian had fled, perhaps to another island. The scary part was that he might return and lure her back to his world of crime. So, Emilie was a friend, but Angela took care what to believe from her, never sure whether Emilie was being coerced into telling lies that might put Jean and his crew in danger.

Angela wound through familiar streets in the city, past restaurants full of lunch-time diners. She parked in front of a two-story building, with a dry goods store on the first level and two flats on the second. Emilie's parents' flat faced the street and included a small balcony. The street was more modest than the one Catherine lived on and there were no flowers on balconies, though the cars parked out front were just as shiny.

Emilie must have been watching from a window, because she met Angela at the door. “My mom’s making dinner in the kitchen. Let’s talk in the living room. We have coffee on. Would you like a cup?”

“Yes, coffee would be great. And sitting calmly with you would we great as well, after dodging crazy drivers.” She chose an overstuffed, comfy-looking couch. “I almost got run over by a huge dump truck.”

“Oh, I know, the commuters seem to have a code of conduct, but in the middle of the day the roads fill up with amateurs.” She poured coffee and sat on a couch opposite Angela. Her skin was pale and she had deep shadows under her eyes.

Angela cocked her head in question and Emilie said, “Last night we got terrible news from the police. A fisherman found Delian’s body on one of the outer islands, washed up on the rocks. His boat was nearby, completely wrecked.”

Angela rose, sat next to Emilie, and hugged her. “I’m so sorry. He took care of you, in his own way, didn’t he?”

Tears streamed down Emilie’s face. “He was a grouch and a prima donna but he protected me. I loved him.”

They remained in a quiet hug, and then Emilie drew a deep breath and wiped her eyes. “Well, I’ll miss him, and I’ll try to remember the good times. Anyway, I wanted you to know.”

“Thanks. I’ll say prayers for him.”

“Okay, that helps. Say prayers for my parents too, okay?”

“Yes. And you.”

The coffee had gone cold. Emily padded into the kitchen, topped off their cups, and returned.

Angela said, “Even though it’s sad times, I’m glad to see you. Do you like your new job?”

“Yes, it’s fantastic. I’m an intern at a sea turtle rescue and rehabilitation center. I get to take care of the turtles, one-on-one. I think they’re going to find a permanent job for me.” She glanced around the room and murmured. “I love my parents, but I’m looking forward to my own flat. I’m moving in with a couple of girls from the center.”

“That’s good news about the turtles. You can still help them.”

"Yes, I'm really happy. I'm glad to see you, too. But you sounded serious on the phone, like you wanted to talk about something important."

"Yes, it is very important, and serious as well."

"Like with drugs?"

"Good guess, and the answer is yes."

"Too bad. They seem to be ruining our island. The two gangs are fighting each other even more than usual."

"Do you still talk with the Dockers?"

She shrugged. "Yes, but I don't do anything for them. Not even look-out duty for police. They respected Delian, and they sort of keep an eye on me on the street, like brothers."

"Do you know Vincent very well? He keeps a boat at the marina and I met him once. He is so intense."

"He sure is. I don't know him well, but we see each other sometimes, when I get invited to watch games on tv with the guys and their girlfriends. He's usually there, like last weekend. He was moody and left before the game was over. Said he had to be somewhere."

"Did he mention any details?"

"No. He keeps to himself about business. Why?"

"There might be something happening here on the island, drug related, and I wanted to learn about it."

"Is Jean involved?"

"Yes, he could be. I figured the more he knew, the better. The drug smugglers have guns. It's dangerous."

"I haven't heard anything, but I'll keep my ears open."

"Thanks. Any news could be helpful."

"I didn't know about Vincent keeping a boat at your marina. I bet it's for drug running. Jeeze, it must be scary, seeing him and his gang members."

"I don't see them often. I guess they leave and return in the dark. Sometimes I hear a boat at sea when I wake up at night. It could be them." Angela paused, remembering. "Once I came across him, stuck in the bottom of his boat. The boat had been sabotaged and was sinking. I jumped on board and pulled him free."

Emilie put a hand over her mouth, eyes widening. "You saved his life? *Mon Dieu*. He'll consider that a debt he owes you."

"That's what he told me."

Emilie patted Angela's knee. "But remember, his gang comes first, no matter what."

"I know. I saw it in his eyes. The problem is, he might have a role in this thing I'm hearing about. The other person is Estelle Boucher. Did you know her?"

"Not really. Only that she had to leave the island. Something to do with the gang."

"Yes, she was close to Vincent. I hear they parted with bad blood, but she might be working with him again."

"You're scaring me, Angela," Emilie's voice was ragged. "Especially about Vincent. Forget the debt. Don't even think about talking business with him. Heck, don't even say hello to him on the street. The man is wired tight and he is lethal."

Angela swallowed hard and changed the subject.

Emilie's mom called from the kitchen, and Emilie murmured, "She'll be asking for help to fix dinner, but she really wants company. Now that I have a job, she misses me."

They cheek-kissed and said their good-byes. Angela mounted her bike and adjusted her helmet, wondering where she could glean more information about Estelle and Vincent. She decided to take a chance at the Central Market.

The place was in its mid-day business calm with local customers but the cruise ship tourists were out in force, mainly looking for souvenirs. A few tourists wore sun hats, others were pink from sun.

She looked for Jean's dad's booth, where the respected *quimboiseur* sold potions that could bewitch or un-bewitch. He was gone, but Angela recognized the woman tending the booth as Jean's mother, Malika.

She beamed when she saw Angela approaching and enveloped her with a warm hug. "My, my, sweet Angela, this is a grand surprise. But you are alone." She pretended to scowl, adding, "That son of mine is not here to escort you and keep you company? I must speak to him."

Angela laughed. "He's working, Malika, saving people from drowning."

"Ha. You have but one life. He must remember the people he loves." She grinned with mischief. "But I speak nonsense. It is only the mother wanting to see her handsome son."

Malika touched Angela's arm and confided, "Jean loves you, girl. I hope you know that."

Angela leaned close and declared, "I do, and I love him to pieces. He is a strong man and he is a sweetie."

"That's just what I tell him. He likes the 'strong' part."

They shared a laugh and Angela said, "I think we both miss him. You're right – he is gone too much."

"Yes, but the sky is blue today and the people are out and talking, so we must take what happiness the Lord bestows."

"Yes, and accept the rest with grace."

Malika nodded. "Well I think that you have come to talk with Joseph about 'the rest', *oui*? My dear Joseph is visiting a client. He'll be back soon if you would like to wait."

"Actually, I think you might be able to help me."

Angela glanced around. Satisfied they were out of earshot of anyone else, she said, "There may be a problem coming to our island. It is not certain, but if it does arrive, we must be ready."

"*Mon Dieu,* Angela, you sound like you are expecting a hurricane. We are just saying *adieu* to one tropical storm, and now a hurricane?"

"Not an actual hurricane, but a storm of a different kind, from evil people who might harm Jean."

"Yes, he only tells us bits and pieces, but I know the danger, the pirates."

"Right, but in this case a very powerful pirate. "It is Bernardo Cabral from Mexico. This man is powerful and very dangerous and I suspect he already has his tentacles here in Guadeloupe. People like this can take over an entire town with bribes and fear."

"I have heard of this man, Cabral."

"So you already know part of the situation. Another part is Estelle Boucher, who you already know. I believe she is connected to Cabral. I am looking for the connection, for information that would be of value to Jean."

Malika's face clouded. "That Estelle is poison. She had her claws into my dear Jean before she left the island in shame. I hope she never returns."

"We ran into her in Paris."

"No!"

Angela explained, including Vincent's possible connection to both Estelle and Cabral.

Malika shook her head in disgust. "If you think she is up to something with Vincent, you may be right. They were thick as thieves, and that gang stuff was what got her kicked off the island, and that instead of jail. You stay clear, okay?"

"But the problem is that Jean has orders to intercept and arrest Cabral. Jean is in danger."

"Not if I can help it. Joseph might have a spell to cast on both of those two."

"That could be a good idea, but right now I'm trying to figure out what Estelle plans to do on the island."

"It's plain to see. She and Vincent will ferry that crook across the ocean, across the island, and into the first plane to China, or wherever they won't just send him back to Mexico."

Angela murmured, "Yes, Malika, but we don't know the details. He can't take a commercial flight. The police will be swarming over the airport."

"I wish I could help. But I don't know anything about Vincent and his Dockers, or that woman." Malika rubbed her cheek. "Except – yes, except that he unloads fish sometimes at the market dock. Maybe that's his cover."

"Really?"

"Yes, in the afternoon. He sells his fish, although there's never a lot of them."

"Maybe," Angela murmured, "he's selling more than fish. It could be that he's distributing the drugs he smuggles to his local dealers."

Malika shook her head. "Then that man is earning a little side money from Cabral, shaving off the top of each drug shipment. Vincent better watch himself on that score or he'll get his proud macho throat cut."

"Maybe I should go to the park next to the dock and take a look."

Malika shook her head. "No dear, you must stay way clear of that man." Her voice was so somber it rose the hair on the back of Angela's neck.

Twenty minutes later, Angela entered a deserted alley near the Place de la Victoire. In deep shadows, she stowed her clothes on top of a fairly clean box behind a dumpster, and shape-shifted.

She carefully kept her paws from touching oily patches on the road but could not avoid the stench from garbage baking in the heat, which overpowered her poor cat nose. She scampered out of the alley and into the sun.

At the dock, fish were displayed on ice in little stands and sold to the locals. A few people hovered nearby. One of the women fishmongers 'accidentally' dropped a tasty morsel of fish on the ground and Angela meowed a thank-you.

She hadn't realized she'd skipped lunch and was hungry. The fish tasted fine. She reflected that a sip of water would top it off, but only a large, dented dog-water tin was visible among the stands, and sharing with a slobbering dog was out of the question.

She wandered the length of the dock, and, to her delight, spotted Vincent's boat. Meandering closer, she saw him in the boat with two other men who appeared to be gang members. They seemed to have completed their business.

One of the men clambered onto the pier and released the mooring lines, then jumped back aboard. The boat curled away from the dock and accelerated into the harbor, leaving a sizable wake from its powerful inboard engine. As she watched, the boat remained stable when crossing a cargo ship's wake, displaying its hardy seakeeping design. The vessel would be very capable of traveling between islands, even to St. Lucia.

As the craft turned and disappeared to the left, on its way to sea, she noticed something flapping in the wind and decided it was a loose piece of the rubber-like matting that covered the cabin and upper hull. As before, she was puzzled why Vincent would wrap the boat with that stuff. There were joints that could leak, it was a boring color, and seemed to serve no purpose.

She made a note to ask Jean.

CHAPTER 25

Estelle was a tangle of nerves as she returned to her seat in the plane, having confirmed with the pilot to land at the small private aviation airport in the town of Saint-François on the south-east coast of Guadeloupe.

Her nerves were all about Vincent. Those many months ago they'd parted on such hostile terms that she had half expected one of his thugs to track her down and murder her. During her first few months in Switzerland, she was grateful to be tucked behind high walls and strong doors.

Attempting to calm her fidgeting hands, she gazed out the window as the plane banked and circled the field. The sunset seemed more glare than color, the single runway appeared woefully short, and the nearby marina, where she planned to land with Cabral, looked too exposed.

With great effort, Estelle cast aside thoughts of the terrible risks she now took – with Maurice, Cabral, and Vincent. All treacherous men. She reminded herself of the prize – rising with Charles on his meteoric ascent to the top of French politics.

Her new stature would bring heightened respect.

And power.

The money? Well, it didn't hurt.

The pilot landed and taxied to the tie-down area. His expression was serious as he lowered the stairway to the tarmac .

"A nice runway and no traffic," he remarked. "It will be rougher in eastern France. Only grass, and likely lumpy. I will check for cows before landing."

Estelle swallowed hard. From this taciturn man, such a cautious observation was unsettling.

Outside, he excused himself to arrange refueling for the return trip to Mexico City and she drew a deep breath.

She hated uncertainty.

And violence.

She gritted her teeth and looked at a row of tied-down planes. Hers was the biggest one, which Vincent would notice but pretend not to be impressed.

His car drew up, right on time, and parked ten meters away. It was the same restored yellow Cadillac as when she was going with him. He stepped out, looking thinner, especially in his face. The pressure of leading a criminal gang, she guessed. Two other men got out of the car and assumed guard positions, facing outward and out of earshot.

Vincent approached. He did not extend his hand. No cheek kiss. Just a pair of dangerous eyes that seemed to look through her as he growled, "I am surprised you dared to return. You left a lot of shit behind. Two of my men are rotting in prison. You might have done some good if you had stayed and helped."

"I wanted to, even with the police closing in. But my parents had other plans and surprised me. They hired a man to kidnap me from my bedroom and take me to a school in Switzerland. The doors of the place were locked from the inside, and judging from the other attendees, it was a sort of mental institution. They taught university classes and bestowed a degree, but it was a prison. I had no money, no phone."

He snarled, "I'm so sad. I'll relay this touching story to the men in prison."

"It's true. I wrote to you but I imagine the letter was intercepted and destroyed by my keepers. I had no money for bribes, or for anything. They even issued us uniforms and toiletries."

"God, Estelle, cut the crap. Tell me what's going on so I can decide whether or not to participate. Right now, I doubt it seriously." He cast her a venomous look. "By the way, where's your security? Just the pilot?"

"No security. On the island, that's your department."

"You trusted me?"

"I knew you'd at least hear me out," she said.

"And if I disagree?"

"Then Bernardo Cabral will remain in police custody."

"What are you talking about? The man is super rich. I'm surprised he's still in Mexico. But that's probably because he's bribed everyone from the president to the janitor and they've decided to drop charges."

She looked around, seeing only the two gang members, the pilot, and a man by a fuel truck hauling a hose to the plane. "We're just going to talk here, out in the open?"

"Yes. It could be a very short conversation. Tell me, how is Mr. Cabral?"

"He is slightly less nervous now that he has hired me to get him out of his villa, past the Guardia Nacional, and to a safe place."

"In that plane?"

"Yes, and your boat."

"Okay, start from the beginning."

Estelle detailed her plans for the route from Cabral's villa to the present airport. She kept mum about arrangements in France and Switzerland, and of course mentioned nothing about her own ambitions.

Vincent nodded with visible reluctance "That all lines up with what he told me earlier today."

"So you have already talked with him." She was relieved and felt marginally safer in the presence of Vincent, incensed as he was.

"Yes, he called this morning and told me that I was to trust you. He didn't mention leaving Mexico."

"Probably because he was afraid the police would be listening in. Have you ever met him?"

"Not in person," he admitted, "but I have met several of his representatives. Greasers from Mexico who spoke high school French. Luckily, we have Latino members who can translate just fine."

"He trusts you."

"I guess he trusts both of us. But, look, he's ruthless. Meaning that he'll waste us if we get in his way."

"But if we deliver?"

Vincent shrugged. "I have to admit, he keeps his word. But there's no margin, okay?"

"I imagine you must adhere strictly to schedule in your work with him. Do you handle payments from the buyer?"

"God, no! I move the packages he sends. They are all sealed. I confirm the count. All I provide is a dependable link on Guadeloupe. So, how in hell did you get him to hire you?"

"He'd talked with other people and I guess he didn't think their plans would work, or he didn't trust them. I think he has a sixth sense about smuggling, whether drugs or himself. He can sniff out weaknesses."

"I'm pretty good at that myself." He glared at her. "Why is it I get the feeling you're not telling me something? What's in this for you? It can't be only the fee, considering you could spend the rest of your life in jail if you get caught. Hell, even if you got away, you could have the police and Cabral hunting you for the rest of your life."

She flashed to those first sleepless nights in the Swiss school, wondering if each footfall on the hall outside her room was a gang member bent on murder.

"You're right. That's why I'm here, to minimize the risks."

He waved a dismissive hand. "No, you're changing the subject. We both know the risks. I'm asking about your private agenda."

She grimaced. The damned man could read her mind. She had to share at least a morsel.

"My private agenda is to move up the power ladder in French politics – diplomacy in particular. I've been consulting for a man named Maurice, and now I want to move up to advising his boss. I've laid the groundwork – "

"Holy shit, Estelle. Who are you working for – the French and Mexicans or Cabral?"

"It's complicated."

"Tell me or I'll drop you like a hot potato."

"Alright, here is my plan. Cabral will escape to a country that will not expedite him. So the French politicians are happy, because they can boast that he his been taken out of circulation and his drug empire has been dealt a death blow – "

Vincent barked a laugh. "That's a crock. Someone else will take over. Probably use my services. Give it three months, tops."

She gestured, "I agree Vincent, but that's how the game is playes, with sound bites and dressed up pronouncements.

Meanwhile, the Mexicans lose a little face because he manages to flee the country, but they figure he's no longer actively making Mexico look bad. And Cabral gets to retire in comfort."

"But the French and Mexicans believe he'll no longer control his global drug smuggling empire? Get serious."

"He will surveilled by France and Mexico, and his communications monitored."

"Big deal, crime bosses can run their business from behind max-security prisons."

"Not in this case. You can believe me or not."

He poked her chest and moved so close she could smell his garlic-laced breath. "Look, sister. You make damned sure he gets through Guadeloupe safely, understood? I want proof that he is in control on that airplane. And just him, you, and the pilot on board. No one else. I want it completely clear to him that I did my part fully."

His entire body shook. Estelle had never witnessed him this furious. Both gang members turned with open mouths, then quickly faced away. She swallowed hard and with difficulty gathered enough spit in her mouth to speak.

"Okay."

He poked her again. "It doesn't end there. I want to hear from him when he gets to his final destination, in his residence, a free man."

Damn, damn, damn.

The man was much more astute than when she left him. He knew he would suffer Cabral's revenge if Cabral were captured at any point before reaching safe haven. Cabral would assert that Vincent knew the full plan, and had ratted him out.

Vincent continued, his lips quivering with rage. "If I find out he was turned over to the police when the plane lands, I swear I will hunt you down myself. I'll kidnap you and take you to Guadeloupe. To a lonely shack in the rainforest on Basse-Terre. I will cut off your right ear. Then I'll let you go in Paris. After a week, I will kidnap you again, and in a dirty basement in the city I will cut off the other ear. Then your fucking nose. You will be a freak when I get done with you."

Estelle thought fast, and concluded that Vincent gave her no choice – *I must eliminate him before I board the plane out of this airport with Cabral.*

One more complication.

She returned his glare, looking him straight in the eye.

But her mouth felt like a desert.

CHAPTER 26

Back at Angela's bungalow, the sun had set and a tepid sea breeze wandered through open jalousies. Boards creaked in the attic, chilling reminders of the grouchy zombie who used to haunt the place.

She washed a plate and a knife.

Thought about another lonely dinner.

Considered what she'd learned that day, and it seemed too little, too late. She debated whether to pour a glass of wine or walk the beach.

Her mobile phone sounded. Jean's ring tone. Steeling herself for more news about him having to remain on duty, she picked up.

"Hi, Jean."

"Hi. You sound sad."

"I miss you."

"I miss you, too. That's why I'm calling. I'm on short notice and have to stay near base, but what about us having dinner at that little place nearby? I'm sorry you have to come all the way in. You were already in the city today, right?"

She smiled broadly. "I'm coming. No worries. Meet you there?"

"Sounds good. Oh, I learned some things today I need to tell you about."

"Okay. Same here."

"I love you, Angela."

"I love you, Jean."

She quickly changed into fresh shorts and top and white strappy sandals, grabbed her safety helmet, and trotted to her TaoTao, humming a jaunty calypso tune.

Half an hour later, she entered the café, made her way to the outside deck, and spotted Jean. He rose from his chair and greeted her with a torrid kiss.

"You look like the cat who swallowed the mouse," he said, sounding a little hoarse.

She chuckled. "Yes, I have news for you, and a question. But why are your cheeks so red, captain? Too much sun today?"

He ignored her jibe and countered with a slow scan of her, from head to toe, pausing at just the right places. Making her blush as well.

They both sat, slowly, eyes glued to each other. He leaned toward her, elbows on the table, and she caught a whiff of his scent. Pictured him without his shirt. Felt her temperature rise.

God, he's a hunk. And he's all mine. Maybe I could sashay over, sit on his lap, and tousle his hair.

He murmured, "I know what you're thinking, Angela."

She snickered, cherishing their shared thoughts, especially these ones, naughty and delightful.

A waitress took their order.

Jean said, "I guess we should talk about the serious stuff first."

"You're right. Are you okay? You have rings under your eyes. You look exhausted."

"I was. Being here with you wakes me up ."

"Me too. I was moping around my kitchen. I'm glad you called." She paused to think. "Okay, on the serious side, I visited Emilie, then your mom – who sends her love and wants to see you more often. Oh, I stopped by the fish pier across from the park and saw Vincent and his boat."

His eyebrows arched. "But you didn't speak to him, I hope."

"Don't worry. I kept my distance. Have you seen his boat? It's made of wood, island style, boxy but seaworthy. And the engine is huge."

"I can imagine. Just right for drug smuggling. Are you suggesting he could be planning to smuggle Cabral from an outer island to Grande-Terre?"

She nodded. "Yes, if he manages to escape Mexico."

"That's what we're thinking as well. I'll be on watch at sea on LA VIOLLETTE, and our Maritime Gendarmerie boat up at Deshaies will out as well."

She nodded, then said quietly, "I discovered something weird about Vincent's boat. There's a gray layer of thin material stuck to the outside of the cabin. On the hull, too, almost to the waterline. I can't iamgine what it's for. Could it be to decrease radar return?"

The waitress brought dinner – fish for both, with island-style French fries.

Jean sampled his fish, his expression thoughtful. "It's possible. Maybe that's why we've only visually spotted Vincent's boat and never by radar. He must have covered the engine, too, because all that steel normally gives a return. Yeah, I think you've hit on something important."

Angela nodded. "By the way, the material has folds in places, and overlaps, and looks lumpy, like it was installed by someone who was all thumbs. I was wondering if a radar reflector might fit next to one of the folds and not be noticed. A little reflector, like the one I have on my boat."

Jean rubbed the stubble on his cheek. "Right, out of sight from Vincent and his crew."

Encouraged by his response, she added, "Maybe attach it to the mast. I could use the reflector from my sloop, and tape it in place, then cover it with a piece of gray cloth that would blend with the radar-absorbing material but let the signal pass through. No one on the boat would notice."

"Good idea." He scowled. "But you can't be the one to mount it, even at night. What if you were caught? There's no telling what Vincent or his thugs would do to you." Perhaps noticing her lips pressed stubbornly together, he took her hand. "It's way too dangerous. No, it's out of the question. I'll have to think this through. Maybe one of my men could attach it."

Angela nodded. What he said made sense, except that Vincent would be suspicious of a stranger messing around on his boat. Ordering a crewman to install the reflector was not the answer. She must do the job, because even if she were caught at least she could claim she was checking the boat and saw what looked like a problem with the material becoming unglued. She could pretend not to know its purpose.

Knowing Jean would never agree, she changed the subject. "Emilie and your mom told me Estelle was headstrong and liked living on the edge, and was close to Vincent."

He chuckled without humor. "I can vouch for the 'headstrong' part, and I've heard that she and Vincent were a couple, and may have been partners in crime. Did Emilie mention whether Estelle had plans to return to Guadeloupe?"

"No, but she might visit if she thinks Cabral will be here. She seems to love being where the action is."

"Sure, for control, and to feel the rush of danger," he muttered.

"Maybe she's already here and keeping a very low profile."

"It's possible," Jean said. "I agree with you that she is up to something connected to Operation Kingfish. Oh, Maurice is on the island and says he's in charge of everything on Guadeloupe to do with Operation Kingfish. He got into a huge pissing contest with my commodore but I'm afraid he won."

She frowned. "Do you think he angled for the assignment because he believes Cabral will come through Guadeloupe, and he want credit for capturing him?"

"Yup. Career enhancing. I'm sure he'll want to be on LA VIOLETTE if there's any chance of us picking up Cabral."

"Maybe he'll get seasick."

"Yes, that's nice thought."

There was little traffic on Angela's return home, enabling her to ruminate on her radar reflector idea. She was convinced that her mounting the device was worth the risk. The reflector would increase the probability of Jean finding Vincent's boat at sea, from 'impossible' to 'certain.'

But her conscience fought the idea, declaring she was breaking a tenant of their trust. She felt a stab of impatience, irked that she had not argued her point at the café. Which caused her to doubt her decision.

An unusual feeling.

She almost never doubted herself, especially at sea, where split-second decisions were needed, like whether to face a wave head-on, or tack to one side and slant up its face. Often, either way would work, but to linger in doubt meant certain failure.

Now she felt doubt.

Was that good or bad? She shook her head – doubt was a useless emotion. Confidence was the emotion she needed to feel, especially in this moment. She consciously chose 'confidence' and resolved to mount the reflector.

With her decision made, Angela felt jumpy with impatience as she arrived home. She leaned her street scooter against a palm tree. Removed her helmet and brushed back her hair.

Inside her bungalow, she finalized her plan, thinking out every step, and the timing as well. She concluded that now, early in the night, was as good a time as any. To wait would be to risk Vincent arriving with a night mission in mind and catching her in the act.

She glanced down the hall at the trap door to the attic, the physical portal to a mystical world. A door through which she had passed, swallowing doubt and embracing certainty. Meeting the zombie on its own terms.

Angela changed to khaki shorts, a worn dark-blue t-shirt and boat shoes. Grabbed a flashlight, screwdriver, black electrician's tape, small scissors, and pliers, and snipped a piece of material from a dark gray dish towel. Five minutes after arriving home, she was racing along the twisty path to the marina, ignoring banches scraping her bare legs.

Angela paused at the end of the path. She surveyed the slumbering piers and their gently bobbing boats, the masts of the sailboats tracing skyward arcs, halyards clacking against aluminum masts. All was in darkness, punctuated by cones of light from bare bulbs mounted at intervals along the piers.

Her steps to the piers and along the planking were silent. Her hands were moist with sweat, her heart pounding. She maintained a steady stride, as if on an innocent errand, mindful of being plainly visible under each cone of light. She arrived at her sloop. As she lowered herself from pier to deck, she scanned for other people and found none.

She shinnied halfway up the mast and paused, gripping the aluminum with her legs. She carefully unscrewed the radar reflector, placing it, the screws, and the screwdriver in the deep front pockets of her shorts.

Back on the pier, she ambled toward Vincent's boat, making sure to look at other boats along the way, pretending to be conducting a routine check. She stopped at his boat as if discovering a possible problem, and swung aboard, placing her feet on the radar absorbing material on top of the cabin.

She moved to the aft-port corner of the cabin top and gripped the short mast, which felt solid beneath its wrinkled coating. Tentatively, she placed the reflector against the mast and shook her head, disappointed. The mast was only about six centimeters in diameter, too skinny to hide the reflector.

She moved forward on the boat, hoping to find a better location for mounting the reflector, one that would provide a three-hundred sixty degree arc of coverage and not be shadowed by the cabin.

The bow was a possibility, perhaps mounting the reflector next to the forward navigation light. But the bow rose only slightly above the rest of the boat, so the reflector would be shadowed by the cabin.

Merde.

Angela glanced about, spotted automobile headlights approaching in the distance, and returned her attention to the skinny mast. It would have to do.

She cut a rectangular section of material from the coating over the mast and placed the reflector in the gap, strapping it in place with black tape. She then taped a rectangle of her gray fabric over the reflector, completing the installation.

Angela glanced toward shore. The car lights were closer, definitely in the parking lot. She held her breath, the sound of a car's engine and crunching tires clearly wafting to her through the night air. She stowed her tape, leftover material, and scissors in pockets, patted the hidden reflector, and turned toward the pier.

The car's lights went out.

Doors opened and slammed shut.

The pier light adjacent to Vincent's boat continued to shine brightly, as if inviting those in the car to look her way.

She stooped, dropped to the aft deck, and undressed, placing her clothes and the incriminating tools inside a gap between rough wooden cabin structure.

In those few seconds, three men had mounted the pier and approached at a quick walk, their conversation loud and clear.

The first man said, “Just a check, he told us. To make sure no leaks or sabotage, plenty of gas, that stuff.”

The second one said, “Yeah, you’ve told us. Let’s get it done.”

The third one pointed toward the aft deck and said, “Damn, it’s a cat. Did you see it? Just jumped from the boat to the pier.”

CHAPTER 27

Bernardo Cabral paced the floor of his study, a room that had witnessed many turning points during his rise to power. Most of them positive. Many with dire consequences to others. All leading to the present moment.

He considered the paneled walls, the vaulted ceiling, the oriental carpets, all fashioned to his taste, imported at great expense. He drew a breath, proud of his creation, and proud to have risen above his arrogant father's business – international trade. Dry and without emotion, without power.

Sounds of movement outside, beyond the villa wall, brought his thoughts back to the coming police attack. His palms were still sweating from the dreaded call he had just received – the police courier, signed warrant in hand, was on his way.

Cabral placed his third scotch of the evening on an eighteenth century Florentine ebony chest and selected a Havana Cohiba cigar. But an unfamiliar emotion tickled his brain.

Horror.

Which, he decided as he snipped the tip of a Chiba, was logical. The reality facing him was police abduction and murder. Or the living hell of solitary confinement in the bowels of a maximum security prison.

"No," he snarled, crushing the cigar in a clenched fist.

He threw the ruined wad at the window. Selected another cigar. Rolled it in his fingers, felt the firm and perfect leaf. Snipped the end. Wet it with his lips and brought it to life with flame. He drew a slow breath, paused, and exhaled.

He loved his villa but now he was impatient to leave what had become a prison with its stone walls, already placing him in solitary confinement.

He pondered. What would his mother advise him in his present situation? Would she criticize his impatience? She, with a soul superior to his in all ways, was the only person whose opinion mattered to him. What would she feel?

Of course, her opinion was not accessible. God bless her in heaven. He crossed himself. No, the only possible emotion in this moment was impatience. Impatience to somehow elude their chafing handcuffs and iron doors and move to a new phase of his life. Brighter. More rewarding.

He stared at a chip of wood in the fireplace, sole survivor from proud logs. He stepped closer, squinting into the shadowed hearth. Half the chip was blackened, but the other half was nearly pristine, untouched by flames.

As was he.

He turned at the sound of an approaching siren. The police, delivering the warrant. Out of the corner of his eye, he saw the door to his study swing open.

Estelle strode into the room, looking chic in black trousers, black blouse, and black running shoes, her normally coiffed hair was tied into a pony tail, a genuinely practical move.

A spot of tan powder stood out on her right shoulder, a souvenir of her trip through the narrow escape tunnel. Rushed through by his chief of security, who had picked her up at the airport. Cabral pictured the German, now making final arrangement with his team in the cellars of the villa.

Outside, the siren stopped, then came sounds of urgent, shouting voices.

Bullets thudded against windows and exterior walls, muted and hollow sounding.

Cabral grasped Estelle's arm and guided her toward the door and into a wide corridor.

"We must leave."

He heard a sharp explosion in the near distance.

Estelle's eyes widened. "What was that?"

"The police forcing the front door. Which is the signal for my security team to set the villa on fire, fueled by your requested explosives and incendiary material."

She nodded grimly. "It will buy you time. The police will wonder if you are in the wreckage."

"Exactly."

He let go of her arm and sprinted with her down the corridor.

Estelle asked, "How much time do we have?"

"Sixty seconds to reach the safe room and tunnel."

"They will still enter the villa, even with the fire?"

"Yes, their blood is up."

The sharp report of weapons firing inside the doomed villa quickened their steps, veering left, then right and down a narrow second hallway. Cabral smiled tightly at the tiny red lights high on the walls, indicating the video cameras were functioning, enabling his security team to time their activation of traps and hidden weapons for maximum effect.

Someone shouted from the direction of Cabral's study. Others responded, and booted feet pounded toward them. Cabral dodged around the final corner, stopped, and pressed Estelle against the wall.

A grenade exploded behind them. Then another, followed by metal shards clattering against marble walls, a groan, and a scream. The explosive shockwave arrived and passed.

Cabral backed away and cocked his head, listening. Twenty paces back, a man shrieked in agony.

Cabral pushed Estelle forward and muttered, "A dozen bayonets now pierce that man."

"Trap door?"

"Yes, slanting toward the center of the opening, tripping the man onto his back and sliding him down. Very sharp points, sufficient to pierce a bulletproof vest. Invented by the Russians."

From behind them, a man shouted orders.

A tendril of black smoke curled from the front of the villa, quickly advancing toward them, expanding from ceiling to floor. Another explosion, followed by heat, singeing the hairs on Cabral's hands.

Hollered commands, and responses of men disoriented in the smoke. Coughing, cursing.

But closer.

"They don't give up easily," Estelle said, her voice tense.

"The traps delay them and put them off balance."

Two rapid shotgun blasts filled the air, the shock wave shaking the fabric of Cabral's shirt.

Cabral hustled Estelle, her hair askew, into the safe room, which was the size of a small closet. He entered beside her and pulled the door shut. Levered four locking lugs into place, creating a six-centimeter thick steel barrier, disguised on its outer surface by hand-carved mahogany paneling.

They moved into a tunnel. Estelle trotted a half dozen meters in front of him, brushing against the wall and glancing back with wide eyes. He followed, praying she would maintain her composure. Her face looked like a twisted mask. Panic hovered close. He caught up with her, touched her shoulder and slowed her to a walk.

He said in a soothing tone, "You did well back there."

She nodded, the motion jerky. "Thanks. I expected more time."

"We are out of their grasp for now."

She gave him a quick look, eyes bright. "No, *Señor*, we are vulnerable. I have planned this moment many times and there is much that can go wrong."

"Oh? Like what?"

"God in heaven! A hundred things. They could be waiting for us this instant, guns drawn, as we run toward them."

"That is not the case. I would have been notified."

"They could be outside in cars."

He shook his head. "Of course. Or hovering in helicopters, or hidden in the bushes. I too have been 'here,' not in my head, but in reality, a dozen times, hunted by police, by my enemies."

She hunched her shoulders and continued forward, appearing frightened and unbalanced by the violence. Cabral admitted that such fright was natural to a certain extent. He would wait for her to recover.

If she did not, he must prevent her from panicking at the wrong moment, exposing him to the police. He would shoot her.

He'd done it before.

CHAPTER 28

A minute later they reached the end of the tunnel. Cabral grasped the steel ladder leading upward. He saw the square of light above, indicating the trap door was open. Taking a breath, he ascended, hoping to hell the police weren't waiting, because then he would be truly cornered.

He poked his head into a small room with bed and chest of drawers, tidy and appearing undisturbed. Cabral's chauffeur, Pablo, stood at the door shifting on his feet.

Cabral growled at him, "So, you thought the police would perhaps emerge from here?"

The man glanced at the floor then said, "The situation is tense in the house, *Señor.*"

Cabral motioned dismissively, turned and gestured for Estelle to join him, then inspected the chauffeur, dressed in one of Cabral's business suits, carrying a satchel.

"Are you ready?"

"Sí, Señor."

"Recite the plan," Cabral ordered.

"I leave here in your car, pretending to be you. If they do not follow, I park and board the yacht of your associate. I change into the uniform of a crew member, here in my backpack. Then I depart in another car, older and more modest. I do not search over my shoulder for police, but act as if all is normal."

"Good, Pablo." Cabral patted his shoulder. "If they pull you over, you are say that you are simply helping out on the yacht, as a crew member. You know nothing of the man who boarded in the suit. You didn't see him. They will hold you for an hour, then release you. I have made a deposit in an account in your name at the small bank you pass on your way to my house."

"I know the one."

"Good. Your job is only to confuse the police and divide their resources of men and communication."

"I understand, *Señor*. I will not let you down."

Cabral extended his hand, they shook, and the man departed. Cabral positioned himself to one side of a curtained window, far enough back not to be seen from outside the house, and watched the chauffeur drive off.

Estelle, by his side, murmured, "No one is tailing him. That's good news."

Cabral shrugged. "Maybe they know where he is going. Or maybe their tail is a block from here, out of our range of vision."

"Yes."

Cabral spoke briefly with the two nervous-looking staff who lived in the house, assuring them of deposits in their accounts and advising them to depart the city, at least, and the country if possible.

After ten minutes, he led Estelle into the garage, they got into a car of modest cost and color, and drove away.

Estelle brushed back her hair and said in a voice still laced with tension, "Do you think the police left someone to watch the house?"

"Hell, I wonder if they even had this place under surveillance."

"They have the manpower. That's their advantage."

Cabral shook his head as he checked the rear-view mirror. "Anything is possible, but even the police have limits. Though I do think they will watch marinas and commercial airports."

"Not smaller airports?"

"Maybe. But not the one we will use."

Fifteen minutes later, as they crossed Mexico City, Cabral answered his phone, listened, and slipped it back into his pocket.

"My chauffeur has gotten to the yacht without incident, changed clothes, and is now driving off in the other car. But someone is following him."

"The police?"

"For sure." Again, Cabral glanced into the rear view mirror. "I see no one following us."

He turned right, entering a storage facility with rows of units for cars or furniture or whatever. He stopped at one and tapped an entry code into his phone. Thirty seconds later, they drove away in another anonymous car, the previous one safely inside the storage unit.

"You know," Cabral said, "I'll bet that damned lawyer tipped off the police."

"You think so?"

"Yeah. I'll bet the police were watching the yacht where Pablo went, and trailed him from there. Probably other yachts as well. He knew all my associates, knew who owned deep-ocean yachts. I'd love to get my hands on that bastard."

"But you think we're okay?"

"God only knows. It's damned fortunate I fired the man before I met you." Switching subjects, he said, "We'll change cars one more time, then go to the airport, like we discussed. Unless you have other ideas, considering what's happen so far?"

"No."

Cabral pictured their destination, a private air strip of a wealthy associate outside Mexico City. The runway was on his ranch, out of sight of the nearest public highway, exclusively for the man's personal use.

He said, "We'll arrive at the airport in about twenty minutes. Your pilot will be there, right?"

"Yes."

Cabral said, "Then we fly south."

"Right, south. Our plan is just as we discussed. We'll report in to air traffic control, using your associate's tail number for ID."

"My associate's tail number? That is a detail you did not share. What if he decides to fly when we are pretending to be him? I don't like this. Air traffic controllers will spot the duplication."

"Don't fret, *Señor* Cabral," she said confidently, apparently putting their explosive escape behind her. "He's on vacation in Germany. His plane is in its hangar, safe and sound."

"How did you penetrate his security?"

"It was not difficult to get inside his hangar. My pilot came with me and made note of the tail number. Look – no more questions. All is fine. My pilot will call Air Traffic Control, file his flight plan to Colombia, and they will assign a transponder code."

"Doesn't the airplane already have its own code?"

"No. The code is four digits long. It's called a 'squawk code,' and lets them track us on radar."

Cabral felt sweat tickle down his spine. "Track us! I thought you said we'd be under the radar."

"Listen, I have all this figured out. 'Under the radar' is an expression. We will be on radar in the literal sense, but we'll be just one of hundreds of other planes, and completely legal and ordinary. A rich guy on vacation, or business, whatever. ATC can check that your associate's airstrip is legal, and is one of many private strips in Mexico owned by companies or individuals."

"What about the tail number of this plane? I own a plane and I am often asked about the tail number as part of the identification process."

"Not a problem. As I explained, we give his tail number. We'll be in the air, where they can't check. Once we've landed, they don't care. Their job is to be sure everyone is safe in the air."

"But if the police decide to double check?"

"And what, send the Mexican Air Force to read the real tail number of every private plane departing Mexico? And not just Mexico City, because we could have driven an hour or two and taken off from a distant airport. No, it's not practical. Besides, you aren't the only person of interest to the police. They have multiple investigations going all the time."

Cabral was not convinced by her fast-talking responses, but forced himself to remain calm. "So, we are hidden in the crowd and we will be in Switzerland before they realize I might be on this plane. Is that is what you are telling me?"

"I'm telling you we are safe." She pulled a burner from her satchel, punched in the pilot's number, told him to complete his pre-flight check and start engines. She smiled brightly at Cabral. "See, it's all set."

CHAPTER 29

Jean's stateroom phone buzzed and he picked up. The clock on the bulkhead read 0105 – five past one in the morning. He had just gotten to sleep.

He identified himself and a voice answered, "Sir, this is the duty watchstander. I have a message for you."

"Alright, go ahead."

"It's marked 'Urgent.' It's in English, from a colonel in the Mexican national police, and the message reads, 'Villa exploded and burned during attempt to serve arrest warrant. Subject presumed escaped. May shift between aircraft and boat. Request you set watch at sea immediately.' Sorry for the pronunciation, sir. My English isn't so good."

"You did fine. My English is pretty basic as well but I caught the drift. The Mexicans want us on patrol."

The watchstander chuckled. "I figured."

They hung up and Jean pressed the speed-dial to Georges, who answered on the second ring, sounding properly formal but sleepy.

"Georges, I've just received a message from the Mexican Guardia Nacional. They lost Cabral. He might have been burned up in his villa, but they assume he's escaped. We need to put to sea. Confirm the crew are all aboard and prepare to get under way."

"Aye aye, captain."

As Jean pulled on his uniform, he recalled the instructions from the thin man from Paris – provide notice before getting underway. Jean had planted his spear about Maurice not being in his chain of command, but chain of command had just been ignored by the Mexicans anyway. They demanded action, not to be delayed by protocol. So he could ignore protocol as well, citing an urgent request by the lead country, which was Mexico.

Though on second thought, Jean felt duty-bound to at least inform Maurice, if only to show cooperation and help keep the commodore out of hot water. But it remained up to Maurice to arrive before LA VIOLETTE got underway.

Jean rifled through papers on his desk, found his notes from the meeting, and punched in the phone number Maurice had given him.

A female answered. “Office of Maurice Blanchette.”

“Good morning. This is Captain Jean Aguillard. I’m calling for Maurice Blanchette please.”

“Oh, hello, captain. This is Anette Laurent. I remember you from the meeting with your commodore. Mr. Blanchette is not available, sir, but I can get a message to him if you would like.”

Jean smiled, because this was the perfect solution. He’d be at sea in half an hour, having obeyed Maurice’s instruction to notify him, and too bad if the man couldn’t reach LA VIOLETTE in time. Maurice’s anger would fall on deaf ears for sure – the Mexicans wanted results and to hell with political niceties.

He said, “That would be fine. Please tell him that the Mexican authorities have informed me that Bernardo Cabral is a wanted man and they have requested LA VIOLETTE assume interception watch at sea immediately.”

She was silent, no doubt thinking through the unsaid part, that Jean was leaving for sea, with or without her boss. Finally, she replied, “Yes, sir. I will relay your message.”

Jean joined Georges on the flying bridge.

Georges saluted. “Good morning, sir. All hands are accounted for, engines warming up, gangway rigged for removal.”

Jean returned the salute. “Very well. Time until departure?”

“Ten minutes, sir.”

The steward arrived with two mugs of steaming coffee.

Deck and engineering sections reported that all was ready for getting underway.

A black sedan Jean recognized as the commodore’s official car sped past the headquarters building, through the shadowed parking area, and onto the pier, squealing to a stop when it reached the gangway.

Maurice, his hair askew and looking even thinner than usual, levered himself out of the back seat. Standing on the pier, he took out his mobile phone, pressed a button and looked up at LA VIOLETTE.

Jean told Georges to hold on removing the gangway. He descended stairs to the main deck, then down the aluminum gangway to Maurice.

Maurice stared malevolently at Jean. "You were ready to leave without me."

Jean looked him in the eye.

Maurice growled. "You are relieved of duty, captain. I will assume command of your little boat."

Jean felt muscles tighten, from gut to face, and his raw anger must have shown, for Maurice stepped back, glanced at the sailors looking at him from the base of the gangway, then at Jean, who was obviously refusing to be relieved of duty.

Maurice said, a tremor in his voice, "You wouldn't dare!"

Jean nodded to the sailors, who dropped the ropes they had been holding at the base of the gangway, and now stared daggers at Maurice.

"Mr. Blanchette," Jean said, "you have just given me an illegal order. Do anything more that impinges on my authority regarding the gallant patrol vessel LA VIOLETTE, and you do so at your own peril."

Maurice drew himself up, lips pressed tight. He glanced at the stone-faced sailors. "Very well," he hissed, "you may continue in your position, but only if you obey my commands to the letter."

Jean leaned close, his anger like a wild animal, screaming for him to throttle the arrogant man.

Maurice's face drained of color, looking haggard in the glare of the pier lights. He glanced at the driver of the sedan, who was staring intently directly forward, hands gripping the steering wheel.

Jean heard a scuff of shoes on deck.

Looked up.

The entire crew lined the rail, fidgeting like they did before boarding a pirate vessel, ready and willing to jump into the fray, to follow him to the gates of hell.

Georges was there, and the chief. Both had strapped on their pistols.

Jean poked Maurice in the chest and spoke loudly enough for all to hear. “I will permit you on board. You are confined to the wardroom. You will enter the bridge or the flying bridge only after receiving permission from me or my first officer.”

Maurice puffed his chest and appeared about to respond, but Jean poked him again.

“And, *Monsieur* Blanchette, if you disobey my orders or those of my first officer, my crew will escort you to our RIB and set you adrift, to be recovered when our mission is complete.”

Several members of the crew coughed.

Georges and the chief made calming gestures to the crew.

Maurice’s response was barely audible. “If you say so, but just wait – ”

Jean poked harder, making the man wince.

“Yes, captain,” Maurice squeaked.

Jean stared into the man’s eyes. “What?”

Maurice’s shoulders slumped. “Yes, I agree, captain.”

Jean yelled, “Louder!”

“Alright. Yes! Fine!”

Jean stood aside and gestured with a welcoming arm toward the gangway. The two sailors let him pass. Maurice boarded and stood on the quarterdeck.

Jean ascended as well, saluted the flag and the quarterdeck watchstander, and boarded. He asked the chief to guide Maurice to the wardroom.

A minute later, on the flying bridge, Jean stepped out of earshot of Georges and the helmsman and speed-dialed Angela. There was no answer. Jean momentarily wondered why, and on a hunch, he descended to the bridge and examined the radar screen.

There were distinct returns from three reflectors. One from a cruise ship moored in the harbor. One several kilometers at sea. And one at the marina where Angela kept her sloop. But that last one was not coming from the pier where she kept her sloop, which was farther from the sea, protected from the open-ocean swells.

The return was coming from a pier close to the mouth of the cove.

Damn, damn, damn.

The headstrong woman had shifted her radar reflector. Taking a terrible risk. Ignoring Jean's wish.

But enabling LA VIOLETTE to track Vincent's boat, day or night, even in rough seas.

Jean was torn between admiration and anger.

He shook his head, and pointed at the luminescent dot displaying the location of Vincent's boat. To the radar operator, he said, "Track this one if it moves. I'll be on the flying bridge, then come back later to check the radar situation."

CHAPTER 30

Estelle realized the next twenty-four hours would be the riskiest of her scheme. To survive, to win, she needed her wits about her. She stifled a yawn and admitted she needed sleep to erase her fatigue, settle her nerves. She shut her eyes and commanded her muscles to relax. Arms, legs, fingers, toes.

She embraced the gentle motion of the airplane.

The serene drone of its engines.

The comfortable lay-flat seating.

The late hour, well past midnight.

But her eyes popped open, stomach muscles tense. She considered a soothing glass of French wine. But that would dull her senses. No, sleep was not coming to her this night.

She sat up and reviewed her notes, mentally tracking their route, south from Mexico City, south-east to Cartagena, Colombia, where they'd refuel, then eastward to St. Lucia.

She looked at Cabral, sitting across the center aisle from her. The plane carried no Cuban cigars, so he was making do with twenty year old single-malt scotch. His eyes were wide open, staring ahead. A twitch in his right eyelid revealed the ragged state of his nerves.

Cabral's mobile buzzed. He picked up and listened, gravely murmured what sounded like 'good bye and good luck' in Spanish, and put the phone back in his pocket.

He turned to Estelle. "It was Pablo, my chauffeur."

"Your double."

"Yes. The police finally pulled him over, still inside the city. They are parked behind him. I guess they're waiting for instructions before questioning him."

"They're being pretty careful. It should be obvious he's alone."

"At this point, it's more about following protocol to the letter. The higher-ups are thinking about the trial, and they don't want their case thrown out because of police misconduct."

"But you said – "

"I know. That I'd never get to trial, much less serve my sentence. But my guess is the stop was made by municipal police, not the Guardia Nacional."

"And they think you're in the car?"

"They must believe it's a possibility, or they'd be questioning him now, spread-eagled against the car."

"How about you being buried in the rubble of the villa?"

He sipped his scotch and swallowed. "No, the Guardia Nacional are too clever to believe that I died in the fire. They'll wait for everything to cool down, then poke through the ashes with a fine tooth comb, but only to be certain. They must have suspected all along that I had an escape plan, and now they'll be searching for a tunnel leading from the ruins, using ground-penetrating radar."

"The same way archeologists scan for buried ruins?"

"Yes."

"But they don't need to wait for the ruins to cool to do that."

He shrugged. "Yes. I'm surprised they haven't already traced around the villa."

"They might have, in the past few days."

"No. If they did, they'd have dug down and gotten men into the tunnel to ambush us. I think they believed they could quickly overwhelm my security team inside the villa with their grenades and automatic weapons, then corner me. They probably made a full-size mock-up of the inside and practiced. Come to think of it, they moved very quickly."

"But your escape worked."

"Right. And here we are, on our way to Switzerland."

Estelle looked him in the eyes. "There is something I need to tell you."

His eyebrows lifted in surprise. "A change in plans?

"No, simply a detail." She smiled. "When we land in St. Lucia, we will be met by Vincent's associate, who will drive us to a yacht."

"They own a yacht?"

She gestured. "No. It's rented, along with captain and crew, supposedly for a island tour. The yacht is very well outfitted and maintained, its owner obviously rich and therefore worthy of respect from police, including the Maritime Gendarmerie . The crew will be dressed appropriately and the captain will be courteous and professional, letting the police inspect the vessel if they ask. It will appear to be just another rich person's yacht, bringing tourist money to the islands."

"But I would be recognized."

"No. Because you will be hidden in a comfortable compartment in an unlikely part of the boat. There you will remain for the short time the police are aboard. But we're getting ahead of ourselves. The detail you must know is that after you board the yacht and we take a familiarization tour and you are shown your stateroom, I will depart."

He tilted his head in question. She continued, "I will return to the plane and fly to Guadeloupe. I must be there to make decisions in case there are surprises."

"But, *Dios mío*, you were just there, making such arrangements."

She raised her hand, quieting him. "There are always surprises, and they will need a quick solution by me on site, not by phone. Besides, there is a risk the plane will be met by police or customs when it lands in Guadeloupe. As a passenger, I will cause no suspicion, but they would recognize you.

"Trust me. Voyaging in the yacht to the south of Guadeloupe, then transferring to Vincent's boat for the rest of the journey, is the most secure way for you to arrive on Guadeloupe. You will be with trusted and knowledgeable escorts at all times."

He raised his hands impatiently. "Very well, we will do this your way."

"I apologize for the extra time involved in riding the yacht, but I assure you it is worthwhile, because of the reduction in risk." Her tone was sympathetic.

He reluctantly nodded. "After we meet at sea, we remain together for the remainder of the journey?"

"Yes. I will be on Vincent's boat when you transfer from the yacht and we will remain together."

He asked, "When will we get to that little airfield in France?"

She released a breath, relieved he'd accepted the arrangement. "Tomorrow, mid-morning."

"But that's daytime. Wouldn't it be better to arrive at night?"

"Definitively not. The runway is no more than a smooth portion of a farmer's field. There may be cows grazing or a bale of hay, or who knows what. Our pilot needs to check it out. Don't worry, it's a sleepy village. We'll give you clothing so you'll blend in as a local, and no one will notice."

He grunted and she continued in a positive tone, as if the whole trip were a walk in the park. "We'll hike through the mountains with a Swiss guide, and a car will meet us on a remote road in the woods. From there, it's an hour's drive to your safe house."

"Which will serve as my base until the estate is purchased and set up?"

"Yes, and the estate is nearly ready for you – the furnished house, the staff, and security measures. All subject to your final approval."

He drew a breath and exhaled. "There are so many details. Opportunities for missteps giving away my presence."

"It is complex but I have done the research, conducted interviews, visited the safe house and the estate."

"Of course. Still, the police are implacable."

She sensed that he was working himself into a state. His eyelid, tranquil for the past few minutes, resumed its fluttering.

She continued, "Remember, we have time on our side, because we are moving quickly, keeping ahead of the police. With distance and time, we expand our possible routes. My gosh, as far as they know, we could decide to go west, or north. They have no clue."

"Or south."

"Yes, but again, they must put their major resources on the fastest route to your destination, which they will likely judge to be Europe, Spain in particular."

"That seems logical."

"It is logical." She paused, suddenly concerned, and asked, "Do you have other places where they might think you would go?"

He stared blankly and she added, "My research indicates the answer is 'no', but I must be sure."

At length, he shrugged. "I have some contacts in China, and have sent out feelers to Japan."

Estelle's stomach cramped. He had paused too long. The damned man was lying. He likely had his own back-up plan, if only a destination or a person.

Which meant there would come a time when he no longer needed her – he would be in a position to make the final jump on his own. What could she do to protect herself? Steal his phone, his credit cards, passport?

No. All out of the question. All she could do now was stay alert and attempt to isolate him from other people.

Mon Dieu! Other people. Like her nemesis, Vincent.

Merde.

She clenched her jaw. Attempted to shake off the feeling of dread.

"Well," she said lightly, "just checking."

Cabral seemed oblivious to her suspicions. As if worried, he said, "As time passes they will come up with no body at the villa and no leads from my chauffeur, then they will look in other directions."

She nodded. "Correct. But by then you will have flown to France, taken a short walk, and be comfortably seated in the safe house. By the way, I've taken the liberty of purchasing top-quality single-malt scotch and Havana Cohibas."

His lips quirked at that last bit, in obvious relish of creature comforts at the end of this harrowing journey. But she knew he'd keep mulling it over, ferreting out the details and probing for flaws. And he'd keep his back-up plan in mind.

She eyed his scotch, and again was tempted to get a glass of wine for herself to soften the tension. As before, she admonished herself to lay off until the work was done.

In even less time than this man envisioned.

He leaned back in his seat, eyelid still twitching, and she considered the known risks in the coming hours. What concerned her most was that final leg to Guadeloupe in Vincent's drug-runner motorboat and the ride to the airport. Not regarding Cabral's safety, but her own survival.

Estelle had read revenge in Vincent's eyes.

Her life depended on Cabral's continuing need for her presence to escort him on the flight to France, the hike, the introduction to all parties involved in his new life and, particularly, to his secure refuge in Switzerland.

Still, Cabral was not to be trusted. What if he and Vincent cooked up a plot to hand her over in exchange for Vincent's continuing help, perhaps through his drug contacts in France? She envisioned Vincent's elation if he managed to keep her behind, as they watched Cabral take off from Guadeloupe. Cabral to freedom, her to face a cruel and lingering death.

She forced herself to focus on the next hours and keep the faith that Cabral would continue to feel dependent on her.

Though the unwelcome idea came to her that Cabral might bribe the pilot. She had been careful not to inform the pilot of their exact destination in France, but it wouldn't take a genius to pick out the village with its grass strip close to the Swiss border. Then came the transfer to a car, the location of the safe house, the names of the security organization, bankers, lawyers.

She had guarded all the details.

But still.

Then there was Charles. She must wait until they were over France, only a few hours from landing, before calling him and informing him that she was handing him Cabral on a silver platter. After her call to him, Charles would have to jump into action on short notice, but her delay in calling him guaranteed word would not leak out, and he would gain credit for Cabral's capture.

Estelle couldn't wait to see Aunt Sabrina's face when she returned to Paris. Though she pondered the scope and risk of those favors to be called in by Sabrina and the Algerian.

She tried again to sleep, but when she shut her eyes, visions of failure loomed – dark shadows, danger, and death.

Estelle breathed slowly, regularly, seeking respite from her doubts.

But the visions remained. As did the need to carry out one other task. She must convince Cabral that she possessed evidence that Vincent planned to alert the authorities as soon as Cabral's plane departed Guadelpoupe. She would give him the name of a competing Mexican drug lord as the person paying Vincent, as part of a plot to take over Cabral's drug empire. She would convince Cabral to have Vincent assassinated immediately after take-off.

Blowing up Vincent in his precious Cadillac would do the job nicely. Certainly, a man could plant a bomb without too much difficulty. Or a sniper could take him out from a safe distance. Cabral would have only hours to make the arrangements, but he could make it happen. Fear and greed always worked wonders.

She pressed her fingers across the inside of her wrist, counting her racing pulse and sweared under her breath.

CHAPTER 31

Angela spent a restless morning working at the marina, her mind only half focused on helping to moor boats, doing paperwork, and briefing visiting sailors on local conditions. And missing Jean.

While sitting on a pier waiting for a sailboat to laboriously tack into the cove and tie up to the marina pier, she called Emilie, hoping for a happy chat.

"*Bonjour*, Angela. I was just about to call you."

"Oh really? My gosh, you sound completely out of breath. Did you buy a fourth-floor condo and just sprint up the stairs?"

"No, we're in the same house, but something big has happened and I ran home to call you. I overheard it at the bar where the Dockers hang out. It's about Estelle – she was back on the island two or three days ago for just an hour, and this morning she arrived again. She's tight as a tick with Vincent! That can't be good, right?"

Angela felt her knees go weak. She squeezed her mobile phone, afraid it would slip out of her sweating hands and fall into the water.

"Emilie, what has happened so far? What did you hear? Did you talk with her? Is this about drugs or Bernardo Cabral?"

"Good – I knew you'd take it seriously. Here's the scoop."

"Wait! Was Bernardo Cabral with her?"

"No, it was Vincent and his top three gang members at a table with Estelle. The rest of the gang were at other tables, and mine was next to Vincent."

"But let me get this straight. Estelle met Vincent three days ago? What was that about? And what airport?"

"Yes, that was the first meeting and it was at that little airport at Saint-François."

"Jeeze, where's that?"

"The airport? It's on the south shore, in the western part of Grande-Terre. It has a marina, too. Anyway, I overheard that Estelle arrived there a day or two ago on one of those business jets, and now she's back. I guess on the same jet at the same airport. Do you think it's about drugs?"

"No. I think it's about Cabral. I wonder if he's on the run."

"There's nothing on the news," Emilie said.

"Yeah, I haven't heard anything either. But if he is on the run, he could arrive soon, or he might have been on that plane and just stayed there. I just don't know. I wasn't sitting close enough to them to hear all the details. But it sounded like they were down to the fine points of some kind of plot. Talking about stuff like who would drive a car. They were excited."

Angela rubbed her chin, trying to put it all together.

Emilie continued, talking fast. "It was like they both understood what the car was for, and they wanted to be sure they chose their best driver."

"How did Estelle look?"

"Sleepy and jittery, but she sounded in control, declaring 'no' for this, and 'yes' for that. Bossy, just like in high school."

"What else did they say?" Angela asked, feeling her heart racing.

"That they were going out in Vincent's boat."

"Did they say why?

"No. Apparently, they'd already discussed that at the first meeting and didn't need to talk about it again. Maybe it's drugs, maybe Estelle is helping Cabral distribute in France."

"Jeeze, could be. Or she's spying for Vincent, listening to all the high-up diplomats and police, and reporting what she learns to him. Did they mention Cabral at all?"

Emilie sighed. "Not by name. Oh, I forgot. They're leaving in his boat soon – this afternoon. He told her it's all gassed up and a couple gang members will be going along. What do you think they're up to?"

"Maybe they plan to transfer drugs and Estelle is going along to oversee the operation."

"*Mon Dieu!* So the drug situation here gets worse."

Angela shrugged. "Sorry to say, you're probably right. I heard from several diplomats in Paris that most of the drugs go to France, but some – more than before – will end up here and on the nearby islands. "

"More gang violence."

"I'm afraid so. Look, my gut says this is about Cabral. Why else would Estelle partner with Vincent after breaking up with him? It would have to be for something important, right? Let's see what we can find out about Cabral, on the Internet and news."

"Okay, and anything I hear on the street."

"Yes, and one other thing – did Vincent and Estelle look like they were back together again, romantically?"

"No way. They were trading mean looks at each other. No small talk, no stories about what they'd been doing while she was away. Just serious business conversation. I don't think they trust each other."

"Like they're working together because Cabral ordered them to?"

"Yes." Emilie laughed. "I bet when whatever they're doing for Cabral is finished, they'll get into a knock-down, drag-out fight."

"Or worse," Angela murmured grimly. "Okay, Emilie. Thanks for this. I need to call Jean and tell him to keep an eye out for Vincent's boat."

They said goodbye and Angela speed-dialed Jean's number, hoping he would be within range, perhaps from a transmission tower on another island. But only his voice mail message responded. She related Emilie's news and wished him a safe trip, wherever he was.

Angela turned her attention to the task at hand, and watched the sailboat she was waiting for make its final tack and come alongside the pier. She helped with mooring, then continued her marina duties, but was on pins-and-needles watching for Vincent and Estelle to arrive.

Finally, at a little past three in the afternoon, Vincent's Cadillac pulled into the marina parking lot. Two rough-looking men got out of the back, stood on either side of the car and glared about. After half a minute, the one on the driver's side signaled. It must have been an 'all clear' message, because the passenger doors opened.

Vincent and Estelle got out.

With one of the men in front, the other behind, they strode quickly down the pier and onto Vincent's boat. Angela's gut ached at the thought of them discovering her hidden reflector. She told her gut to calm down, and headed to the workshop.

Knowing she was plainly visible, Angela forced herself to walk slowly along the piers with her head turned from Vincent and Estelle. To be recognized by Vincent wouldn't be a problem. He was used to seeing her at work there. But if Estelle spotted her, and she recognized her from Paris, there would be big trouble.

Angela arrived at the workshop, said hi to Michel, who was bent over his workbench examining what looked like a pump. He nodded vaguely and she continued to her cubbyhole office. She opened the single window. Moving fast, she shut the door and slipped off clothes and shoes and stowed them in a desk drawer, then shape-shifted to a black cat. She felt just as nervous in her feline form.

And even more nervous when she recalled that she'd left clothes on Vincent's boat from her last shape-shifting. What if they were discovered? Would Vincent think strangers had borrowed his boat for a quick tryst, or would darker thoughts come to mind? At the very least, such an invasion of his turf would make him more vigilant than ever.

Mon Dieu – forget the nerves. She would just go to the boat, give a little listen, then figure a way to relay anything of interest to Jean as soon as possible.

She jumped up to her desktop, then to the windowsill, paused a moment to gather herself, then bounded down to the ground. She trotted along the piers to Vincent's boat and hid behind a piling, poking her head out only far enough to survey the boat.

Back on the aft deck, Vincent and Estelle were speaking in urgent tones, and up forward two gang members were on deck preparing for sea. Angela edged closer, picking up Vincent and Estelle's conversation, just audible above the swells lapping against pier pilings.

Angela willed them to reveal the purpose of their trip, whether drugs or Cabral, but was disappointed.

"We'll be out for hours," Estelle said with an edge to her tone. "Do you have sufficient fuel?"

"We have plenty of fuel on board," Vincent snapped impatiently.

"Just checking."

Which sounded like an apology. Very odd, from the bossy Estelle.

They continued to talk, but someone on another boat turned on a radio and music blared, drowning out the pair's conversation. Angela crept closer to Estelle and Vincent but that didn't help. She moved along the pier toward the center of the boat and bounded aboard. Swaying to the gentle roll of the boat, she traced her way through the open back of the cabin and hunkered down in the shadows on the port side.

She still couldn't catch what Vincent and Estelle were talking about.

CHAPTER 32

Angela bided her time. She wriggled off a deck splinter that was poking her back legs, and was licking a front paw clean when she heard one of the gang members, now serving as deckhands on Vincent's boat, step onto the aft deck.

He paused.

She lay perfectly still, a black furry shadow among other shadows in the dimly lit cabin. Hopefully, invisible.

But he pointed. "Hey! We've got a stowaway!"

She tensed, ready to startle whoever dared to grab her and leap off the boat.

Vincent walked aft, his shoes stopping only centimeters from her nose. He looked down. "It's a freaking black cat."

The deckhand mumbled, "Black cats are bad luck, boss. Want me to toss it off?"

"Leave it," barked Vincent. "We've got work to do. Let it look for rats. Probably a couple on board, from all the half-eaten sandwiches you two leave around."

"Uh, okay. No problem. Anyway, we're ready for sea. Fuel topped off. Lines singled up."

"Good." Vincent strode to the control console, fiddled around, muttered, and the engine rumbled to life.

Angela realized she had only seconds to get off the boat. She glanced around, making sure the way was clear. Vincent remained at the controls, Estelle sat aft on the transom, and the deckhand who wanted to toss Angela overboard was engrossed in coiling a line.

Angela gathered herself to leap to the wide gunwale, and from there to the pier.

But the deckhand clomped across her intended path, forcing her to scoot aside. He climbed over the gunwale and onto the pier, where he lifted a line from a cleat and tossed it onto the aft deck, forcing Angela to dodge again, then he shouted above the roar of the engine, "Lines clear, fore and aft, boss."

"Alright," Vincent said, and he put the engine in gear and turned the wheel, pivoting the boat away from the pier.

Angela sprinted aft, where the distance to the pier remained jumpable. But she had to evade Estelle's feet as the woman strode toward the cabin.

With her way again clear, Angela sprang to the top of the transom and crouched for her leap to the pier.

The engine suddenly roared and the boat jerked forward, causing her to lose balance as the gap widened to an unjumpable three meters.

Angela caught her breath. There was no way she could make the leap. She wondered if she should dive into the water and swim ashore.

But as a cat she hated water.

The deckhand spotted her and gaped. "There's that stupid cat. No rat in her mouth. I'll throw her overboard, see if she can swim."

Vincent ignored him and pressed the throttle full forward, causing the boat to plane on the smooth water of the marina. The deckhand lost his balance and grabbed a handrail, eyes wide.

Now, Angela had no choice. She had to remain aboard, and her first priority was to find a safe refuge, in the shade and away from sea spray and these clumsy humans. She walked into the cabin and surveyed the exposed side-hull structure of wooden stringers and ribs.

One spot looked suitable, located a little less than a meter above the deck, with a horizontal stringer that was wide and long enough for her to lie flat. She would be protected, yet able to see and hear all the activity within the cabin. Angela bounded up and made herself comfortable, remaining alert for possible new information from Vincent and Estelle.

Both of the men sat on the foredeck, talking, and Estelle moved close to Vincent. She made a show of looking toward the bow, then from side to side, and said in feigned innocence, “My gosh, Vincent, it’s the same boat as before. You’ve moved up since then, and you own a magnificent car. Why this tired old boat?”

He glared. “As I have told you many times, she is seaworthy, and her engine runs on gas, not diesel – compact and strong.”

Estelle raised a hand in mock surrender. “Yes, but what is this gray shelf paper doing, plastered all over the outside?” She poked the top of the engine casing. “No, it’s not paper at all – it’s cloth, very fine threads.”

“Yes, metallized polyester, cut to shape and applied with adhesive to all the external surfaces of the boat. Can you guess what it’s for?”

Estelle’s eyebrows arched, likely chagrined that he’d gained the upper hand in this little tiff, and she scoffed, “Certainly not beauty. You could have at least chosen a tropical color.”

His response sounded harsh to Angela, a bully’s laugh. “Ha! It only comes in gray and brown, and gray blends with the ocean.”

“Okay, then why?”

“To absorb radar from the police and the competition. Makes us invisible until close range when they can see us, and even then we look small.”

“Hmm, and innocent, like you’re just a local fisherman?”

“That’s the idea, yeah.”

“Well,” she said, her tone full of doubt, “the Maritime Gendarmerie will be out there. We’ll see how it works this afternoon.”

Vincent grunted, checked side-to-side, and navigated through the entrance of the cove. The swells in the open ocean caused the boat to roll, and Vincent slowed, making about ten knots, Angela figured. The rolling motion continued as they progressed. That told her they were perpendicular to the seas, which moved from east to west. So, they were heading south. Perhaps to meet a boat, or journey to another island, for drugs or Cabral.

After he steadied up on a southerly course, Vincent asked Estelle, “Who’s the pushy guy from Paris? My sources say he’s a diplomat. He arrived this morning and was picked up by a Maritime Gendarmerie car from their base in the city.”

“God, Paris? Do you have a description?”

"Tall and thin. My contact said he was intense, like he had a broom handle stuck up his ass."

"Jesus! It's Maurice. He used to be my boss. Still is, I guess. I tried like hell to keep him off Guadeloupe, but here he is, sniffing around. He'll want to take credit if Cabral is captured here."

Vincent scowled. "He sounds like a snoop with lots of authority. Could screw up our plans."

"Don't worry, he knows nothing about what we're doing. He can't interfere." In her bossy voice, she declared, "We move forward exactly as discussed."

"No, sweetie." He laughed harshly. "Things have changed. My fee just doubled. Guys like Maurice can bully the local officials, threatening them with consequences from Paris if they don't help him. Who knows what he'll tell the Maritime Gendarmerie to do? He could even order a special army unit from France or police from the nearby islands. Hell, there'll be more boats and planes and helos searching for Cabral. The risk is way higher now." He pounded the steering wheel. "What a cock-up."

She patted his arm. "Don't worry, I've got everything under control. First, I have taken advantage of flaws in the French-Mexican team's capture plan. Also, I have a strong relationship with Maurice's boss. As soon as we're back ashore with Cabral, I'll call him on my mobile phone, and get him to order Maurice back to Paris. End of problem."

Vincent gave her a long, searching look. "Why would Maurice's boss help Cabral escape?"

"He won't."

"Except, he will let him leave Guadeloupe?"

"I think you're getting it. So calm down, okay?"

"God, you're devious."

Angela wished it were a simple drug run with Vincent. She could handle him. But adding Cabral and Maurice was like pouring gasoline on a fire. She was attempting to thread the needle, keeping Cabral invisible as she shepherded him to Switzerland.

But the possibility of confrontation was astronbomical.

And none of the participants – including Jean – would give an inch.

She could have used that calming glass of wine about now.

CHAPTER 33

On LA VIOLETTE's flying bridge, Jean raised his binoculars to blood-shot eyes and scanned the coast of Basse-Terre, looming ten kilometers to port, its towering volcano plainly visible.

The sea glared in the late afternoon sun. Jean rotated his gaze south, then west.

Georges, asked, "Anything?"

"Just cars driving along the coast highway. Nothing coming out to sea. How about you?"

"The same. Everything looks calm. A few sailboats. Oh, and a cruise ship approaching from the south. Where do you suppose Cabral is?"

Jean shrugged, lifted his coffee cup, downed the last bitter sip and replaced it in its holder. "We know he escaped from his villa about ten o'clock Mexican time. The distance from Mexico City to St. Lucia is about four thousand kilometers according to our charts. If he's got a private jet, cruising at eight hundred kilometers per hour, he could be here in five hours, which would have been about five this morning."

Georges nodded. "Maybe longer, if their final leg to Guadeloupe is by boat, say from Martinique or Dominica. Anyway, airplane, then boat, then another airplane from Guadeloupe sounds way too complicated to me. Seems like we, and Chief Lambert up at Deshaies, are wasting our time bobbing around out here."

"I agree," Jean said, "considering all Cabral's other options. I wouldn't be surprised if he were in an airplane, headed anywhere but east, then by some roundabout route to his final destination. Spain or some other European country, to lay low."

Georges looked into his coffee cup, shook his head and replaced it. "I can spell you if you want to get some sleep. Looks like a long day, and maybe the night."

"No, but thanks anyway. Maurice wanted his own stateroom, so I loaned him mine. He's probably sleeping or reading, which is fine with me because he's out of our hair."

"He's obnoxious," Georges muttered.

"True. A pain in the ass. I'll have to wake him if we ever do spot Cabral, then he'll second guess everything I do. Besides, if Cabral is coming by boat, the window for his passage to Guadeloupe opened this morning and could last a day or even more. I want to be standing right here if he shows up. Sleep is a luxury at this stage."

Jean glanced at the cruise ship, which was taking a jog to the west of Basse-Terre, heading north.

He said, "I'm going below to check the radar picture. I don't want to miss anything that might be hiding between us and Basse-Terre in this afternoon sun."

"Aye, sir."

"*Monsieur* Garnier has the deck and the conn."

The helmsman made eye contact. "Aye, *mon capitaine*."

Jean set his binoculars in their case, descended one level, and entered the bridge. He approached the pedestal-mounted radar display and greeted the operator.

They both gazed at the flat rectangular display, dominated by a black circle in which yellow dots depicted ships and green masses showed land. Jean recognized Basse-Terre, the dots of several small craft and the cruise ship he'd spotted through his binoculars. There were no vessels shown in the area where the sun glare masked his vision.

When Jean had familiarized himself with the various vessels' courses and speeds, he asked the operator, "Is there anything that looks suspicious – maybe a boat that could be carrying Cabral or is behaving oddly?"

"Not yet, sir." The man nodded at the display. "You can see several small craft, a couple with radar reflectors, the others fairly weak. The largest contact, other than that cruise ship passing up the west coast of Basse-Terre, was a steel-hulled inter-island cargo ship. She's continued north, out of our range, headed for Pointe-à-Pitre."

The operator pointed. "Oh yeah, there's this contact you told me to track. It produces a strong return, no doubt with the help of a radar reflector. Probably a fisherman." He scratched his chin. "But that's odd – her speed is twenty knots. On her way to a particular fishing ground? It's going fast, particularly over one-meter swells. Probably rolling quite a bit."

"Then why's she going so fast?" Jean asked in an innocent tone, knowing full well it was Vincent's boat.

The operator looked at Jean and must have spotted his grin, because he smiled as well. He asked, "Does she remain a contact of interest, sir?"

"Yes," Jean said. "I'm certain I know that boat, island-built and owned by a gang leader named Vincent Ballou. She's wooden, but she has a radar reflector – that's the reason for the strong return. Now the question is, where is she going?"

The operator generated a black line, easily visible against the blue of the screen, and attached it to the contact. The line, showing the vessel's course based on her present heading, extended in a southerly direction, into the open water south of Basse-Terre, and not intersecting any of the southern islands of Guadeloupe.

Both men stared. Then the operator pointed to another contact, placed a cursor on it and tapped his keyboard. Another black line appeared, denoting a northerly course.

The two lines crossed.

"Do you think?" the operator muttered.

Jean felt a rush of energy. "Yes – given their speeds and headings they're on an intersecting course. Track both contacts."

"Aye sir." The operator paused a moment, then said, "Sir?"

"Yes?"

"The first contact came from a small marina on the south shore of Grande-Terre. It departed just over an hour ago."

Jean wanted to be doubly sure, and asked, "Which marina?"

"The chart names the bay, 'Port de Saint Félix,' but I didn't see the name of a marina."

Jean's swallowed hard. That was indeed where Angela moored her sloop. And Vincent moored his boat. His suspicions were confirmed.

He let out a breath. “She did it.”

“What, *mon capitaine*? Is there a problem?”

“No, if my hunch is correct. I believe that boat is en route to pick up Cabral from this other contact. The boat is very fast and nearly invisible to radar. But a woman I know has mounted a radar reflector, enabling us to easily track it.”

“*Mon Dieu!* This, er, woman – ?”

Jean was certain of the man’s real question, because everyone seemed to know that he and Angela were serious. He responded, “Angela Spencer.”

“She is quite brave, sir.”

“Yes. And impetuous to the core.”

I pray to God she is safe.

Looking away and wiping an unexpected tear from his eye, Jean strode to the captain’s chair at the starboard side of the bridge and lifted a microphone. He pressed a button labeled ‘flying bridge’ on his communication console and waited, gazing south, where their other contact was fast approaching.

The first officer answered. “Flying bridge. *Monsieur* Garnier.”

“Georges, sound general quarters. We have a suspicious pair of vessels on radar. I’ll be right up.”

Outside, he ascended the steps two at a time, the general quarters gong in his ears.

Haunted by a fearful question – Did Angela get away unseen after she mounted the reflector?

CHAPTER 34

Angela gagged from the stinky bilges of Vincent's boat. Covering her nose with a paw didn't help. Nor did breathing through her mouth. She muttered a prayer for Jean, hoping he was tracking them at this moment.

If there was only something she could do to help him.

Merde.

She grumped, then rose and stretched her back legs, and jumped down to the cabin deck. Traced her way around Vincent's and Estelle's feet, and made her way to the aft deck. Avoiding the wave spray on the foredeck, the two crewmen were seated aft, their backs against the transom, chatting and smoking. Cigarettes, she thought, but weed it turned out to be, when she caught a whiff on an eddy of wind. The deckhand who wanted to throw her overboard made a half-hearted grab at her, which she easily dodged, then they continued talking.

She found a spot a few meters from them, snug against the starboard side and shaded from the late afternoon sun. As before, the boat was mainly rolling, indicating a continuing southerly course, with Grande-Terre behind them and Basse-Terre off to starboard.

A minute later, Vincent slowed the boat to a crawl. He barked an order, and his crewmen trotted to the foredeck, where she heard shouting, as if in greeting, followed by a back-and-forth exchange. With her interest piqued, Angela arose and ambled into the cabin. Vincent stood at his usual place at the wheel, with Estelle at his side. Both looked through the windscreen at something out of Angela's range of vision. She bounded onto a narrow shelf at the base of the windscreen and followed their gaze.

Only a hundred meters distant was a sleek modern yacht, about forty-five meters in length, constructed of white fiberglass with glistening stainless steel trim. The vessel rolled in the swells as she approached slowly, then came to a complete stop and rotated to present her stern, on which was painted her name, ESMERELDA.

Vincent aimed at the stern of the yacht, his deckhands on the foredeck setting bumpers and throwing two mooring lines to crewmen on the yacht. When the distance between the vessels closed to ten meters, Vincent slowed even further, and stopped completely when his boat was a meter from the yacht. The two vessels bumped lightly, now positioned bow-to-stern.

He gestured to Estelle to follow him, and led her to the foredeck, holding her hand to steady her against the motion. Vincent's deckhands and two crewmen on the yacht helped Vincent and Estelle to a diving platform spanning the yacht's transom, then up a built-in stairway to the aft deck.

A stocky man that Angela recognized from photographs as Cabral shook hands with Estelle. He appeared drawn and pale, apparently seasick or nervous. He cast a dour glance at Vincent's boat and spoke to Estelle. She shook her head and he grimaced, likely not thrilled with the ongoing transport arrangements.

Vincent, Estelle, and Cabral retreated into the superstructure, and the yacht's crewmen moved out of sight, forward. The yacht remained, having swallowed up Estelle, Vincent, and Cabral, and providing an answer to the question of drugs versus Cabral. For sure, Cabral would transfer to Vincent's boat for the onward journey.

Now was the time to act, with all of them together, cooped up at sea. Angela gazed hopefully at the radio, which appeared similar to the one on her sloop. But she needed to be a human to operate it, and Vincent's two deckhands remained planted and wide awake, lounging in the shady cabin.

Then they stirred, and strolled aft and began to pee over the transom. Desperate to help Jean in the coming conflict, Angela shape-shifted into her human form and grabbed her clothes from their hiding place in the cabin structure. She quickly pulled on khaki shorts, dark-blue t-shirt, and boat shoes, all wrinkled and smelling of splashed-on bilge water. She checked pockets, finding flashlight, screwdriver, black electrician's tape, small scissors, pliers, and the remainder of the dark gray dish towel she'd used to disguise her radar repeater, seemingly a year ago, but only three days before.

She glanced hopefully at the radio, but the men had finished at the transom and were returning. She had run out of time, and her only choice to flee to the yacht. An idea formed on how she could help Jean – cause a distraction. A big one. Like sinking the yacht. Anything to give him time to arrive on the scene. She dodged out of the cabin, desperately casting about for ideas as she fled to the foredeck. She decided that sinking the yacht through her sea cocks would take too long. What else could she do?

But they were coming for her.

She focused on getting away, gaining time and space to think. They were almost on the foredeck as she tugged the mooring line, bringing Vincent's boat closer to the yacht's diving platform.

She leaped aboard, but they they were two steps behind her, now laughing as if this were a game. She quickly ascended the stairs to the aft deck of the yacht, and decided her only hope was to get to the engine room. She could certainly do some mischief there, if only throwing circuits to cut power.

But there was no time to seek the right door. Her only hope was entering through one used by the others. She would then seek a passageway leading forward, and find a way to descend to the bowels of the vessel to the engine room. She sprinted to the door and flung it open, the two crewmen only a few meters behind her, their heavy breathing and taunting insults loud in her ears.

She passed through the doorway.

Entered an air-conditioned space.

And collided with Vincent, Estelle, and Cabral, standing in a tight group. They froze, conversation stopped, and time seemed to stand still for a split second. She desperately searched for a way out, catching details of the space, its lush white carpet, stuffed chairs, coffee tables, and a bar. Cabral held a drink; the others were empty handed. All three gaped at her.

The split second expired. Not surprisingly, Estelle was the first to speak, ordering Vincent's men to return to the boat. They got the nod from Vincent and departed.

Cabral shouted, "Who the hell – "

Estelle shrieked, "You're that girlfriend of Jean's! You tart! What do you want now? How did you get here?"

Vincent glanced at Angela, his expression puzzled, and said to Estelle, "She's the manager of the marina. How do you know her?"

Estelle pointed an accusing finger at Angela, "She's a friend of Jean's."

"Jean Aguillard?"

"Yes! The damned captain of LA VIOLETTE."

Cabral gulped his drink, then spluttered, *"¡Jesus, Maria, y José!* She is a connection to this Aguillard! She is *peligrosa*. Dangerous. Throw her overboard! She must be in communication with him."

Estelle raised her hands, commanding silence. "A radio in those tight shorts? I think not. I am certain she is alone and out of touch with Jean or anyone else." She gazed at Angela in triumph. "And she is now our prisoner."

"But – "

"No, *Señor* Cabral. She is no danger at all. She is our bargaining chip with her boyfriend."

She spit out the last word, chilling Angela, now furiously doubting the value of all her snooping, and the damned reflector. Worse, she had become a terrible liability to Jean's mission.

Vincent turned and looked her in the eye – for a moment too long.

Estelle stared at Angela and stepped close, smelling of stale sweat and perfume, her hands shaking with rage. She poked Angela's shoulder, as if assuring herself she was real, and not a ghost appearing out of thin air. Apparently satisfied, she stood back and smirked, the skin of her face taut, eyes wild.

She hissed, "Why the devil you poked your nose in our business, I haven't the faintest clue. But this I know for sure – your presence will constrain your besotted boyfriend from pursuing us, much less shooting at us." She turned to the men. "The Maritime Gendarmerie have ceased to be a threat."

Angela lifted her chin. "Not so fast, Estelle. You are still in deadly trouble. Jean is on his way and he will do his duty to capture all of you." She made eye contact with each of them in turn. "You should surrender now."

Estelle shouted, “Ha! He is a Frenchman in love. No longer a danger to us. But I am a mortal danger to you. You are now a witness to a private affair. I trust you understand.”

Angela met the woman’s poisonous gaze. “You are threatening to kill me.”

“No, I am not threatening; I am promising. Your end will be long and painful. I will use a garrot, and I will look into your pleading, bulging eyes. With pleasure.”

Cabral appeared surprised and pleased. Likely, the man had passed such dire sentences on drug competitors and carried them through. To him, Estelle’s response must have sounded logical.

Vincent’s face was a blank, but his eyes gleamed with emotion. Again, he looked at Angela, but this time only for a split second.

CHAPTER 35

Standing on the flying bridge, with LA VIOLETTE at flank speed, her sharp bow cleaving through rollers on its southerly course, Jean soon spotted a white blur where radar predicted the southern-most contact would be. In the following minutes, the blur morphed into a large yacht.

He muttered to George, at his side, "Do you see the other contact?"

"No, not – wait!" He pointed directly at the yacht. "Yes, and they've joined up, see?"

Jean squinted through his binoculars. "Yes, moored bow to stern."

Jean picked up his microphone and announced, "All hands, this is the captain. Set general quarters. Prepare for armed boarding and inspection."

Weathertight doors clanged open and shut. Men sprinted along decks. The mounted guns forward and aft were armed and checked, and the RIB readied for immediate launch. Readiness reports streamed in.

LA VIOLETTE was prepared for action.

There was a scuffle behind him, and Maurice appeared, followed by the chief petty officer, who said, "This man entered the bridge without permission and started issuing orders. Said he had taken charge."

Jean turned, his blood high, and Maurice blurted, "Men were running about in confusion. You were nowhere to be seen. Someone had to take charge of the vessel."

Jean addressed the chief, "Thanks, I'll take it from here. You may go to your GQ station."

The chief saluted and departed. Jean turned to Maurice, noted the warning expression on Georges' face, and said, keeping his tone even and correct, "We have just identified two craft meeting at sea, one from Guadeloupe and the other from points south. They could be meeting to have a chat, but we suspect they are transferring Cabral for transit to Guadeloupe and beyond. The activity you have remarked upon was my crew going to general quarters in readiness for possible armed conflict. You are not to interfere in any way. Is that clear?"

Maurice's face reddened. "I shall inform my superiors."

"Feel free to do that. Meanwhile, I will update my commodore, who is my superior, and I will proceed as ordered by him."

Maurice glared.

Jean continued, "This is a Maritime Gendarmerie matter. Leave the flying bridge. Stay out of the way."

Maurice stiffened as if struck. He released a quick breath, opened and shut his mouth, and departed.

Jean called through to the commodore and described the situation, concluding with, "We are proceeding at speed with an estimated arrival at the two vessels within twenty minutes."

The commodore asked, "Have you briefed the diplomat?"

"Yes, sir. He is attempting to contact his superior. He might have a satellite phone. We have not made our communications facilities available to him."

"Very well."

"Presently, we are at general quarters and are prepared to conduct an armed boarding."

The commodore paused, then said, "I understand. Your orders are as before – ascertain whether Cabral is present on the boat or yacht, and if so, arrest all persons from both vessels. Use deadly force if necessary to protect your personnel and vessel and to capture or otherwise stop Cabral. That man must not escape."

CHAPTER 36

Angela, painfully aware that the three people facing her were capable of murder, declared to Estelle, "You are wrong."

Estelle snapped, "You pipsqueak! How dare you address me like that. You have no clue what you've stumbled into."

A door at the forward end of the salon opened and a man in white uniform with captain's epaulettes strode to the group. He addressed Estelle.

"We have a boat in sight, heading our way at high speed."

"You are sure? Aiming at us and not another destination, perhaps beyond our position?"

"I am sure. We have been tracking it and several others during our approach to the rendezvous. The others are going their own ways and will not pass near us, but this boat has been acting differently. It has been moving in the area east of Basse-Terre, with no apparent destination. Until twenty minutes ago. "

Vincent asked, "Is it the Maritime Gendarmerie ?"

The captain nodded. "I believe so. I am not so familiar with the vessels of Guadeloupe, but it is the shape of an armed police patrol boat."

Vincent said to Estelle, "It's LA VIOLETTE!"

Estelle asked the captain, "When will they arrive?"

"I calculate they will be alongside us within ten minutes."

She nodded curtly. "Remain on the bridge and do not respond to calls from LA VIOLETTE. After their second call, turn your vessel bow-on to the patrol boat. That will get their attention."

"But that – "

Estelle shook her head. "Just for a moment, then turn broadside, stop your engines, and surrender. We'll take care of ourselves."

Looking chagrinned, the captain saluted and departed.

Angela cleared her throat and said to the others, "I realize you have planning to do and would just as well have me out of earshot. Would you mind if I answered a call of nature? It's not like I can escape."

Estelle waved a dismissive hand, "God, woman, take all day if you want. *Les toilettes* are just outside the door the captain used."

Angela exited the salon and entered a passageway leading toward the front of the yacht. She ignored the door marked 'Toilet' and stopped at a door labeled, 'Crew Only.' After a furtive look over her shoulder, she opened the door enough to see a descending steel stairway and hear the muted thunder of the vessel's two diesel engines.

Carefully, keeping eyes peeled for crewmen, she crept down the stairway, thinking out her next step – how to create that diversion.

Entering the overheated engine room, the answer popped into her head – fire, the most feared of all maritime calamities. She needed oily rags and a way to set them afire. She scanned the compartment, which spanned the width of the yacht and ran twice that distance fore and aft.

She reached a lower-level walkway, serving engines, pumps, electric switchboards, and other equipment. All were painted white and spotlessly maintained. She found an alcove with a workbench, along with shelves holding clear plastic cases containing bolts and small fittings. There was an electric receptacle on the bulkhead.

To the left of the workbench stood a multi-drawer tool cabinet, and to the right, a red metal wastebasket with a latched metal top. Undoing the latch, Angela peered inside the wastebasket. As expected, it contained discarded oily rags – flammable material.

She peered all around, seeing no crewmen, but discovering two CCTV cameras, one forward and one aft. Both no doubt with wide-angle lenses that encompassed the entire engine room. She calculated she had about two minutes before someone on the bridge discovered her and showed up asking all the wrong questions.

Angela pulled her screwdriver from a pocket and unscrewed the faceplate on the electrical receptacle, then the junction box inside, coaxing it into the open, being careful not to touch the live wiring. She reached into the wastebasket and grabbed a bundle of oily rags and placed them on the workbench. Then she tipped the wastebasket over, emptying the rest of the rags onto the deck.

Above the tool cabinet she unlatched two steel doors, revealing an array of cans. Moving quickly, she selected a spray can of solvent and doused the rags on deck. Behind her, the diesels continued to rumble at idle speed.

A door slammed, above and forward, and footsteps clanged on steel stairs. Someone was on his way to investigate.

Using screwdriver and pliers from her pocket, she released positive and negative power wires from the junction box, pulled an oily rag close, and touched the wires together. Crackling white sparks appeared, igniting a flame, which enveloped the rags. She pushed the burning rags off the workbench and onto those on deck. The entire collection caught fire and belched acrid smoke.

Suddenly, the engines roared, turning twin propeller shafts. Angela jumped at the sound, fearful she had accidentally pressed a throttle or gear engagement lever, then remembering no such controls were within her reach. It had to be a command from the bridge.

Did that mean they were trying to run from an approaching LA VIOLETTE?

Impossible to say.

The fire caught further; smoke billowed, and she coughed.

Ten meters away, up forward, a crewman appeared, yelling and running toward her, then pausing to grab a portable fire extinguisher. He brandished the extinguisher and screamed, his words swallowed by the diesels' racket, but his intent obvious. She ran to her steel stairway and scurried up.

Reaching the passageway, she locked the door open, and smoke began to drift from the engine room. She heard a loud ringing, figured it was the fire alarm, and spied a door to the weather deck. She pushed it fully open and clicked it in place, pulling a draft and strengthening the flow of smoke from her fire. She was set to run forward on the vessel, hide until Jean arrived, then jump overboard and swim to LA VIOLETTE.

But a hand gripped her arm. Estelle! Pulling Angela back to the salon, where smoke was emerging from the ventilation system, stinging Angela's eyes.

Vincent and Cabral stood by the door leading to the aft deck, both looking anxious to leave.

Estelle shoved Angela toward them.

Angela knew she could overpower the woman, her own muscles strong from working on her sloop and around the marina, but she also knew Vincent would grab her in a second, and she was no match for him, so she allowed Estelle to guide her toward the door.

Cabral opened the door, causing more of a draft to pull smoke into the salon, and he motioned for the others to follow. On deck, Vincent looked at the smoke billowing stronger from the open door and set a restraining hand on Estelle's shoulder.

"We need to buy time or they'll catch up with us!"

She gave him a puzzled look.

He nodded toward Angela. "We leave her. To lighten our load and increase speed."

"No! She must come. Her weight will make no difference."

He briefly turned to Angela, away from Estelle, and mouthed, *"Merci."*

Angela nodded, understanding – one word, his thanks for a debt, a life for a life, now being repaid in full.

To Estelle he said with authority, "This one as well as my crew will stay behind."

Estelle growled, "No! I will kill her!"

Vincent, the merciless gang leader, got into her face and snarled, "Then you and she will both be captured by the Maritime Gendarmerie ."

Cabral had disappeared aft. Estelle glowered at Angela and followed him, with Vincent at her side. Smoke swirled, screening them from view.

And Angela stood alone.

CHAPTER 37

When LA VIOLETTE approached within a hundred meters of the smoking yacht, Jean ordered 'all-stop' and turned parallel to the other craft. He called the yacht's bridge on VHF Channel 16, the international distress frequency, but received no response. He hailed the vessel with a bullhorn, but still no response. Yet, uniformed figures were plainly visible in the enclosed bridge.

Jean was elated to have trapped the two vessels, and was certain that Cabral was still aboard the yacht. Likely, Vincent was as well. And Estelle, perhaps. He assumed Angela remained safe ashore, having done her bit in enabling him to track Vincent to this rendezvous.

Georges abruptly turned from sweeping the vessel with his binoculars, and pointed. "He's getting underway. See the prop wash back aft?"

Jean nodded. "Damn, you're right!" He ordered, "Bow gun, fire a shot over his bow."

The gun fired, a geyser of white water rose in front of the yacht.

Georges said, "Sir, he's turning his bow to us. *Merde!* He's going to ram us!"

Jean ordered, "Bow gun, single shot to their bridge. Both guns, prepare for concentrated fire to their bridge. Bridge, hard left rudder, starboard engine full ahead, port engine full astern."

He waited as LA VIOLETTE pivoted, her bow coming around to meet the still-turning yacht, bow to bow. Jean was positioning for a passing maneuver, though, because of the vessels' proximity, would likely result in a hard side-to-side scrape.

As LA VIOLETTE continued her pivot, Jean caught sight of movement aft of the yacht. *Mon Dieu!* It was Vincent's boat, aimed away from the yacht, throwing a huge white wake, and racing for Basse-Terre, only a few kilometers away. He counted three people aboard, grouped in the open cabin.

The yacht continued to turn, her bow now pointing directly at LA VIOLETTE. Jean was an instant from giving the command to fire both guns when the yacht stopped her rotation and wake boiled at her stern – not behind the vessel, but folding back upon itself.

Jean said with relief, "She's stopped forward motion, stopped turning."

As if underlining his words, the yacht's captain appeared on the starboard bridge wing and spoke into a mike in French, his voice coming over Channel 16. "Yacht ESMERELDA calling Maritime Gendarmerie patrol boat. We surrender."

Jean picked up his mike and replied, "Yacht ESMERELDA, this is Maritime Gendarmerie LA VIOLETTE. Disengage your engines. Prepare to receive boarding party."

"Yacht ESMERELDA to LA VIOLETTE, message received. We will comply."

Jean ordered, "Bridge, hold position parallel to the yacht, one hundred yards distant."

Still on pins and needles, Jean joined Georges in scanning the yacht, probing for any signs of armed resistance. The captain remained outside and visible, and two of his crew attached a boarding ladder over the starboard side.

Jean turned to Georges, who he'd assigned to lead the boarding party. "She looks safe enough, but take care."

George saluted, "Aye, captain. Good luck with catching the others."

CHAPTER 38

Jean aimed his binoculars at the fleeing boat as LA VIOLETTE turned to an interception course and accelerated to twenty-eight knots, their top speed in the active seas.

A minute into the chase, George called and reported all was well on the yacht and they were proceeding to base, towing the RIB. He tentatively continued, "Captain, there was, um, another person on board."

"What?"

"Well, er, a woman."

"Georges – "

"Captain, it's Angela. Don't ask how. She just walked onto the bridge. She's fine. Here, I'll pass her the mike."

Jean was torn between elation that she was safe, and anger that she had put herself in mortal danger. He took a calming breath.

"Hi, Angela. Are you okay?"

Anger must have crept into his voice, because she paused a beat before replying, "Um, yes."

"Angela, did you put the radar reflector on Vincent's boat?"

"Yes. And I set the fire, too."

His voice caught and it was his turn to pause. "Angela, you are one of a kind."

She read him perfectly and responded with a chipper, "I know, captain. So are you. I love you."

Wincing at all this being on an open line during a combat operation, and figuring 'what the hell,' he said, "I love you, too. Look, I'll see you soon, okay?"

Her voice turned serious. “You need to catch Cabral, and Vincent and Estelle.”

“They’re all on the boat?”

“Yes.”

“Thanks, Angela.”

At first, Jean was cautious about getting too close to Vincent’s speeding boat, and he set a parallel course, offset by two hundred yards as he caught up. His chief concern was rocket-propelled grenades – RPGs. That is, if Vincent had any onboard. Pistols and rifles were not an issue because they were effective only at closer ranges, lower speeds, and over smoother water.

But as LA VIOLETTE pulled even with the boat, he concluded that Vincent probably did not have an RPG aboard. If so, he would have at least chanced a shot by then, to force his pursuer to slow down and open the range.

‘No-RPG’ was good news, but the trouble was, the distance to shore had dwindled to a kilometer, much too close for Jean’s comfort. Cabral could swim the final meters if they waited much longer.

Using binoculars, he scanned through the open back of the boat’s cabin and counted three people. They appeared to be staying put, not even using a hand gun to shoot back, much less a rocket-propelled grenade launcher. Vincent must have been counting on speed alone to win the deadly race, even if he did have firearms aboard.

Jean hailed the boat on VHF Channel 16, but received no response, as expected. He scanned the boat again for other people, certain that Vincent would have brought several gang members along for line handling and defense. But he must have left them on the yacht, and released Angela as well, who they could have taken as a hostage. All to lighten their load and attain maximum possible speed.

He remembered passing what looked like the top to a wooden structure during the chase, and through his binoculars he had identified the floating object. It was the cover to the boat’s inboard engine. Vincent would likely have thrown off other gear. Come to think of it, Jean had spotted three semi-submerged red gas cans. The man was desperate.

For an instant, Jean wondered about Estelle, born and raised on Guadeloupe, 'graduating' to international crime at the highest level, and now poised to lose it all. The last of a series of bad choices, he reflected.

Jean had no intention of letting Cabral get away. If they surrendered in the next minute, fine, Cabral and the other two would be captured with no bodily harm. Otherwise, 'deadly force' would be their demise. He ordered the bow gunners to fire a shot over the boat's bow. Jean knew the stern gun's arc-of-fire was blocked by LA VIOLETTE's superstructure, so he exercised only the forward gun, the larger of the two, at twelve-point-seven millimeters.

The gun boomed and the round landed fifty meters in front of Vincent's boat, which sped unhindered through the resulting splash, toward shore.

He ordered, "Fire on semi-automatic until target destroyed."

The gun fired in three-shot groups, the individual shots blending into a sharp ripple, then the next group, all finding their mark on the hull or within several meters of the craft, the gunner gaining and then holding his target, in spite of the constant motion of LA VIOLETTE and the evading boat.

Vincent chose not to weave from side to side in the usual defensive tactic, but kept his bow aimed at land. Jean spotted a half dozen men waiting on shore, and three cars parked on the Basse-Terre coastal road.

Just as Jean was making a mental note to attack those men on shore after dealing with the three on the boat, one of the three-shot groups from his bow gun struck the fleeing boat's gas tank. Gasoline huffed, vaporizing in a foggy cloud, followed by an explosion and a massive fireball.

The explosion ripped hull and superstructure to pieces. The engine appeared as a solid unit for a second, then descended into the sea, pressed by the shockwave above. As the fireball dissipated, the debris field became visible, composed of floating bits of wood emitting yellow flames. Roiled water, cast aside during the explosion, resumed its place, banishing flames. Bits of wood and a scorched life jacket bobbed to the surface.

Jean trained his binoculars toward shore, but the people and cars were no longer there. He ordered LA VIOLETTE to pass through the explosion site from two directions, and saw no evidence of human remains.

He ordered the crew to stand down from general quarters, then he moved among them as they stowed unused ammo and gathered shell casings. He shook hands and complimented all, whether on deck, below in the engine room, or on the bridge. He reflected that they had merged into a single, coordinated unit, and together faced the stress of combat. He was proud to be their captain.

CHAPTER 39

Angela remained outside and aft on ESMERELA, standing vigil with Georges' military binoculars. She scanned the sea off the southeast corner of Bass-Terre, where the air was now clearing from a huge explosion, the sound of which had reached them as a hollow rumble.

Georges had assured her that Jean radioed a brief after-action report that the fleeing boat had been destroyed in the blast, and all personnel on LA VIOLETTE were unharmed. 'All unharmed' was well and good, but she needed to get her arms around Jean before she could banish her fears for his safety.

Mon Dieu! She had been through an emotional ringer herself, and threatened with an agonizing death by Estelle.

Yuck.

The guys from Jean's patrol boat, being guys, had bypassed offering sympathy for her ordeal, and instead clapped her on the back and made her retell the story of setting the fire, during which they openly admired her courage and ingenuity. She guessed that was what guys always did after a dangerous mission.

In truth, although she missed their symapathy, she relished their compliments, because they had often faced life-threatening danger with their own courage and ingenuity. They knew.

One of Jean's crewmen confided to her, "You'll find that each time you recount your adventure, you will weave in more danger and daring, eventually making the tale larger than life. It's a *sea story*, Angela, and its purpose is to entertain and amaze, needing only a kernel of truth." He laughed and so did she.

Come to think of it, in their own rough and tumble manner, the crewman, and even Georges, did sympathize with her, but in a very different way. A way in which they demonstrated a love of being alive and having bested a frightful situation. They had inducted her into their special circle. Their ultimate accolade.

Now, grinning, she scanned the sea again, and this time she spotted a gray blur that grew in size and form, with white smudges on either side, revealing LA VIOLETTE and her twin bow waves, speeding to meet them.

When the patrol boat caught up with ESMERELDA, the two vessels slowed and maintained a hundred-meter separation. After five minutes, Georges joined her. Several others walked aft, to where the RIB was being towed.

"Is everything okay?" she asked.

"Oh yes, all's fine. We'll proceed together as we return to base, just in case there's any, er, lingering problem in the *engine room.*" He grinned at the gentle jibe and she shook her head in mock dismay. He continued, "We'll heave-to and transfer the RIB back to LA VIOLETTE so it can be safely stowed on deck." He paused, with a twinkle in his eye.

She pretended to be worried, but both knew it was an act, and she asked, "Well, what about me?"

He pretended to be surprised, then grinned and said, "Oh yes, you will ride the RIB as a special passenger." He chuckled. "The skipper would court martial me if you weren't aboard."

They laughed, and feeling the yacht slowing, they looked across to LA VIOLETTE, also slowing, until both vessels were only moving sufficiently fast to maintain steerage. She made her way to the swim platform, where the crewmen gave her a life jacket and helped her board the bouncing RIB.

Jean met her after the short trip between vessels, and immediately escorted her to the flying bridge. They were alone up there, with the chief below in the bridge, now maneuvering in parallel with ESMERELDA, bows pointed toward their base in Pointe-à-Pitre. A light breeze ruffled their hair and the sun was low over Basse-Terre.

Leaning on the bulwark, their shoulders touching, Angela felt the tension in her chest ease, and holding hands with Jean, she could feel him calming as well, if for only these precious minutes, shedding the burden of command. They had kissed, then for long minutes, they were silent, both as one in spirit, emerging from danger, back to normalcy.

At length, she asked quietly, "They're all dead?"

"Yes. It was fast. One moment they were alive, speeding to land, with escape only seconds away, and the next moment, swallowed in – "

She put a tender finger to his lips. "Don't. It happened and now it's over. Let's be thankful that you and your crew are okay."

He forced a smile. "And you. You made the capture possible by mounting the radar reflector. I knew exactly who to chase. And the fire – what was that all about?"

"I wanted to distract them."

She moved very close, feeling his warmth in the cool late-day breeze.

He looked into her eyes. "Hmm, like now?"

"Yes. I am very good at distracting you as well."

She kissed him, for the first time noticing the bristle of whiskers, evidence of his remaining on watch throughout the previous night and day.

She asked, "What will happen with the diplomat, Maurice?"

"I spoke with him briefly. He was badly shaken. I took him to the wardroom and gave him a stiff shot of cognac. Amazingly, he thanked me, and he asked me to stay for a while.

'"He said he had changed his mind about me and my way of melding the crew into an effective force capable of stopping Estelle, Cabral, and Vincent. He admitted that he'd never seen such a chase and deathly explosion in person, and told me his report would include positive words for Guadeloupe's Maritime Gendarmerie. Toward the end of our discussion, he poured me a cognac, and more for himself, and we toasted."

"Do you think he's really changed?"

"A part of him, yes. He witnessed the lethal capability of his government, beyond diplomacy, and he was smart enough to recognize that."

"But, you think he'll still reach for more and more power?"

"I think so, but maybe with maturity."

"How about the captain and crew of the yacht?"

"I've spoken with the captain, and there will be a formal enquiry. He told me he thought ESMERELDA was being hired for innocent inter-island touring. Only after they got to sea did he learn something fishy was going on, though he was never told that laws were being broken. He really got worried when Estelle and her crowd were getting ready to leave and Estelle ordered him to turn his bow to LA VIOLETTE."

"Do you believe him?"

"Yes, but I want to verify. That's the purpose of the enquiry."

They were silent, but only for a minute. Jean turned to her, gazed into her eyes and placed a hand on her shoulder.

"Angela, I love you so much. I want to be with you always."

"I love you too, Jean. I was worried sick when I saw the explosion, even after Georges assured me you and your crew were unharmed."

He wrapped his arms around her and she pressed into his embrace. She wanted him to never let go, but too soon he stepped back. He looked down at her and smoothed her windblown hair, his eyes kind and strong. Her heart quickened.

"Angela Spencer, will you marry me?"

She flung herself back into his arms, tears in her eyes. "Oh Jean! Yes, yes, yes. I will marry you. You are my love. I could have lost you this afternoon. What if they had a – what is it?"

"A rocket-propelled grenade," he said, choking back emotion. "I had thought you were safe ashore, but all that time you were their prisoner. And that damned Estelle – "

"She said she was going to murder me in a horrible way."

"So close, Angela."

"We both could have died."

The statement hung in the air, punctuated by a seagull cawing above, the muted rumble of engines.

He was such a brave man, yet vulnerable. Together they'd faced so many dangers but they had survived.

"We'll make our own world," he whispered.

"Yes. A safer world for ourselves and maybe – "

"For our children?" he said, his eyes bright with passion.

"Definitely lots and lots of children," she teased.

They kissed to seal their vows. She smiled and so did he, his special smile that was full of fun and energy and love just for her, as the sun set, the air chilled, and the lights of Pointe-à-Pitre welcomed them home.

ABOUT THE AUTHOR

As a boy living on St. Thomas, Jonathan Ross learned to sail, then went on to explore the US and British Virgin Islands. He climbed rocks along the rough coast, stepped on sea urchins, and watched shooting stars on dark Caribbean nights. He loved the sea and all the boats that sailed upon her, but mostly the sea. Years later, after service in the Navy, Jonathan laid his mother to rest in the Caribbean Sea outside of St. Thomas Harbor. You may visit Jonathan at Facebook.com /jonathanrossnovels and at jonathanrossnovels.com.

A final word – If you enjoyed this book, please consider posting a review on Amazon.com. It really does help, and your feedback is greatly appreciated.

www.ingramcontent.com/pod-product-compliance
Lightning Source LLC
Chambersburg PA
CBHW070834120626
46556CB00002B/752
* 9 7 8 1 9 6 7 8 5 4 0 1 1 *